Claire Barker studied English literature, history and illustration. Previous careers have included being an astronaut, a wizard and a poodle groomer. Married with two daughters, she lives in a heavenly corner of North Devon, inventing fantastical nonsense and avoiding the hoovering.

Magical Mail

Written and illustrated by Claire Barker

Boxer Books

First published in Great Britain in 2010
by Boxer Books Limited.
www.boxerbooks.com

Text and illustrations copyright © 2010 Claire Barker

The right of Claire Barker to be identified as the author and
illustrator of this work has been asserted by her
in accordance with the Copyright, Designs and Patents Act, 1988.

ISBN 978-1-907152-58-0

1 3 5 7 9 10 8 6 4 2

Printed in Great Britain

All of our papers are sourced from managed forests and renewable resources.

2 the 3 of you,
4 your faith in me

Contents

Chapter 1

'Faith is a crybaby'

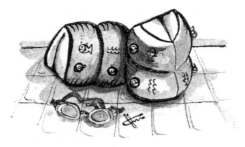

If there was one thing you could say with absolute certainty, it was that Faith Smyth was no hero. She was rubbish at running, terrible at tennis and rotten at rounders. She wasn't very brave and much preferred a nice, safe book to climbing a tree. She was shy and quiet and fell over a lot. In fact, if you blinked, you might miss her completely.

This would have been no big deal in an ordinary family. But unfortunately for Faith, her family was anything but ordinary. They were extraordinarily ambitious, extraordinarily beautiful and extraordinarily talented, not to mention loud, sporty and competitive. They even had a family motto: 'No Pain, No Gain'.

They were all super achievers – Mr Smyth was a brain surgeon and Mrs Smyth was a kick-boxing instructor with her own business called 'Fighting Fit'. Faith's big sister Victoria was a regional beauty queen finalist and her little brother Tristram was preschool chess champion. But the only thing that Faith was really good at was losing her hair-slides and forgetting her PE kit.

"I don't know *where* Faith came from," her mother would sigh despairingly, "she's just so… different."

Holidays were a nightmare. Water sports were always top of the Smyth family agenda: swimming, surfing, sailing and scuba-diving. Victoria and Tristram would perfect their life-saving techniques while Mr and Mrs Smyth powered up and down the pool doing butterfly stroke. And Faith… well, Faith would cling doggedly to her armbands at the shallow end, as invisible as ever.

One summer they decided to go pony-trekking in the Welsh mountains. Whilst the rest of the Smyth family cantered fearlessly into the distance, Faith stayed back at the stables, chatting to the ponies about her interesting pebble and bottle-top collections.

Eventually Mrs Smyth decided that some less sporty activities might help Faith fit in. She arranged a family trip to Pendragon Castle, knowing that Faith was interested in 'that sort of thing'. When the day came, Mrs Smyth enthusiastically packed her handbag with clipboards, pencils, a whistle and a stopwatch. She insisted that these items were absolutely necessary to ensure that 'Team Smyth' completed the castle quiz in record time.

Unfortunately, within ten minutes of arriving at the castle, Faith began to feel anxious about bats getting caught in her hair. Grumpily, the whole family trudged back to the safety of the car.

"Faith's spoilt it *again*," said Victoria, examining her immaculate nails.

Tristram piped up, "Faith is a crybaby."

"*Shush,* you two!" said Mrs Smyth, eyeing them in the rear-view mirror. "Please be more POSITIVE." But it was clear that she agreed with them as she drove home, grinding her teeth.

The next day Mr Smyth decided that it was "just silly nonsense" and all Faith needed was some "quality time" to get her back on track. So he scheduled an hour with her between his morning golf lesson and lunchtime power-swim.

He took her to a café, bought her a milkshake and solemnly asked her how she was. Faith spent fifty-eight minutes talking about a scary dream she had had involving a bat in her hair. After this Mr Smyth decided that quality time with his daughter was "not necessary" but that he definitely needed some "me time" urgently.

School wasn't exactly a bundle of laughs either. Faith Smyth was a child who was overlooked by just about everyone. She was the quiet one who played alone in the playground. The one who sat there all lesson, not really knowing what to do, but feeling too shy to say anything. The one who wasn't naughty enough to be noticed, but wasn't clever or funny enough to be noticed either. She wasn't *desperately* unhappy, but sometimes she did feel a bit lonely.

Thank goodness she had Bus Bear for company.

Bus Bear was a tiny blue teddy bear, sent to her by her dad's Great-Aunt Hope as a christening present. He had been special all her life, so he was a bit worn around the edges.

Faith kept Bus Bear in her school bag in case of 'emergency loneliness'. This all began when she had nobody to sit next to on the school bus, hence the name. She was very careful to keep him a secret, because she thought the other children might laugh if they found out about him. Victoria and Tristram certainly did.

Of course, she would have liked a special human friend more than anything, but everybody was in a gang already, so that was that. It was a shame, because Faith was kind and loyal. She was patient and thoughtful. She was fair and generous and lots of other wonderful things.

But how would anyone know? How would anyone know when nobody ever took the time to find out?

Chapter 2

Expect the Unexpected

But one Tuesday, everything changed.

It had started like any other Tuesday. Mrs Smyth began the day with yoga, chanting and a bowl of wheat-free, dairy-free, fat-free grains; and Mr Smyth drank a smoothie made of fish oil and kiwi fruit. Victoria had been up since dawn, moisturising tirelessly, and Tristram had beaten his computer at chess again. Faith's hair looked like seagulls had been fighting in it and her school jumper was on inside out.

"Quickly, quickly, my darlings or you'll miss the bus," chirped Mrs Smyth brightly, scrubbing yesterday's mashed potato off Faith's school skirt. If anything she sounded a little *too* bright, but she had been reading *Be a Positive Mum* and she was determined not to sound cross (even if she did have to wear special guards at night to stop her wearing her teeth down from the continual grinding).

As usual, Faith sat on her own on the bus. When she was sure no one was looking, she reached inside her bag for Bus Bear. She fumbled around the pencils, half-read paperbacks and forgotten newsletters, but he wasn't there. She began to fret, until she remembered that she had been reading a story to him last night before she went to sleep.

Faith loved stories, all stories of all types. All tales, short or tall, long or little. When she was reading a story she could lose herself in other worlds full of dragons and mermaids, kings and treasure. A good story made everything better. Of course! She had left Bus Bear tucked in her pillowcase with a dog-eared copy of *Magical Myths*. 'Sugarlumps,' she thought. 'Never mind, I can manage without him for one day.'

When Faith got to her classroom, her teacher, Mrs Troublebottom, wasn't there. It wasn't long before someone came in to tell them that she had been struck down with a sudden case of mystery measles. Faith's heart sank. A teacher on sick leave only ever meant one thing – chaos.

There was already a lot of shouting and throwing of bags going on and everybody was sitting in different seats to their own. Faith didn't like it when this happened because it was difficult to find somewhere to sit. It was always, "No, you can't sit here, I'm saving it for a *friend.*" And this time was no different – Faith found herself moved around again and again until she ended up sitting next to Josh Plunkett, a boy known for his tendency to pick his nose and pinch people. The noise was deafening as pencil cases flew through the air like zipped-up birds.

Amid the anarchy the classroom door opened. Slowly, soundlessly, a tall man in a white suit glided in. Like a shutter coming down, a hush fell upon the children.

The man spoke quietly but firmly. "Good morning, children. My name is Mr Lancelot, but you may call me *sir*. I am your supply teacher for the day. Now, if you will all kindly return to your correct seats – and I do mean your *correct* seats – we can check the register."

It's hard to say exactly what was so special about Mr Lancelot, but he sort of *glowed.* All of the girls went moony-eyed and the boys suddenly became very well behaved. He was certainly handsome, with very smart clothes and a voice like melted fudge. But hang on a second! How did he know that they were in the wrong seats?

Before Faith could figure this out, Mr Lancelot began to write something on the board. In big chalk letters he carefully and deliberately wrote:

EXPECT THE UNEXPECTED

Then he smiled to himself and sat down. Settling his hands on the desk, he looked down at his long, elegant fingers. The seconds ticked by. Everyone looked at each other expectantly till eventually he spoke.

"I need a volunteer. A brave, clever, capable volunteer. Oh, yes, and they must also be of noble heart."

Twenty-eight hands flew up. Even Josh Plunkett took his finger out of his nose to fling his hand in the air. The only hand that wasn't raised was Faith's. What was the point? She never got picked anyway. It was a fact of life. Mrs Troublebottom always picked Jasmine Squire, with her pony club rosettes, or Francis Fleming, with his tidy hair and shiny shoes.

Which is why it was so remarkable that Mr Lancelot, without even looking up from his desk, said quite clearly, "Faith. Faith Smyth. Would you come here, please?"

Everyone looked shocked. Some even looked disgusted. No one was more surprised than Faith. As she approached the desk, Mr Lancelot looked up and fixed his sparkly eyes on Faith's brown ones and smiled a delighted smile.

"Ah, my dear Faith. How good to see you. Could you deliver this package to the caretaker's office, please?"

Opening the bottom drawer of Mrs Troublebottom's desk, he drew out a bulky brown envelope. Gingerly, Faith picked up the packet and turned it over in her hands. No name, no message. She turned to leave.

"Oh, and Faith –"

Faith looked back over her shoulder "Yes, sir?"

Suddenly he stopped smiling and looked very serious. "That parcel is only to be delivered by you, do you understand?"

Faith nodded. "Yes, Mr Lancelot. Only by me."

Chapter 3

Emergency Courage

'Wow. He was a bit odd,' thought Faith, secretly feeling thrilled that the supply teacher had picked her.

As she walked down the corridor, she had a funny thought. Mr Lancelot hadn't even read the register yet, so how come he knew her name? And what did he mean by it being 'nice to see her'? Actually, she was sure he had pronounced her name strangely as well. But before she could dwell any more on these oddities she arrived at the caretaker's office.

She knocked on the door. No one answered. She knocked again. Still nothing. Reaching out, she turned the handle, but it was firmly locked.

'Typical,' she thought to herself. 'My first errand ever and it goes wrong straight away.'

Faith turned to leave and was halfway down the corridor when she heard a noise.

RAT-TAT-TAT RAT-TAT-TAT.

Looking back over her shoulder, she saw a red letterbox in the very same door she had just knocked on. And not only that, but it was flapping furiously.

RAT-TAT-TAT.

Faith didn't remember seeing it there before.

RAT-TAT-TAT!

The rattling was getting louder and louder, so cautiously she walked back to the caretaker's office, clutching the parcel to her chest. She looked around but the corridor was empty. By now the rattling and flapping was frantic, so, in an effort to muffle it, she pushed her parcel through the hole. With a loud creak, the door slowly swung open.

Faith was beginning to feel a bit scared. Warily, she stepped inside. The room was dark, echoey and smelt of damp mops. In the far corner was a desk, on top of which was a lit candle. In the pool of light cast by the flame, she couldn't help but notice crumbs on the floor.

"Um... hello? Is anyone there?" Faith's voice was a bit trembly but she ventured further into the gloom.

'I'll just leave this on the desk and go,' thought Faith. Tentatively, she walked forward and stretched out her arm to put down the parcel. Then she noticed a letter in the flickering candlelight.

It was no ordinary letter, for all of the words were made up from bits cut out of a newspaper. Faith looked over her shoulder but nobody was coming. Did she dare? Just a quick peek. She peered a little closer at the letter. It was addressed to the editor of *The Times*!

Dear Mr or Mrs Editor-person,
I am enclosing ten letters that I have stolen from their owners which will shock and aStound your readers. They expose the magical, the mythical and the fantasticall aS Fakes! Shams! Phoneys! As ordinary as bread rolls!

Finally the time has come to show the world what these faiRY tale fraudsters are realLy like!
   In exChange I want a car, a house, a giant chOcolate cake, a dancing penGuin, a (hang on, I've got to get some more newspaper out of the recyCling bins...)

An anonymous ransom note! Faith noticed a pile of letters on the chair next to the desk. They must be what the note was going on about. She picked them up, dusted off more crumbs and quickly scanned through them, her eyes widening in astonishment.

They belonged to *real* pirates... witches... mermaids... dragons... the Big Bad Wolf... But this was terrible! Why would someone take their letters and try to spoil the magic for everyone?

'This person must be stopped!' she thought to herself. The letters needed to be returned to their real owners before the newspapers got hold of them!

But what could she do? She thought about telling her family. Then quickly she changed her mind. What about the police? No, they'd think she was crazy. She tried to think of someone noble and courageous. What about Mr Lancelot?

As his name crossed her mind she noticed that the parcel she was supposed to be delivering had a message on it, written in scrawling green ink.

For the urgent attention of Faith Smyth

Well, *that* hadn't been there a minute ago.

Suddenly Faith had a funny feeling. It was the sort of feeling that starts at the top of your head and drains quickly down to the bottom of your shoes. It was *not* a particularly pleasant feeling.

As she gingerly tore open the corner she revealed a blue furry paw, then another. Then a tummy and an arm and a shiny, black button eye until... there he was, sitting in her hand – Bus Bear! Tied around his neck was a parcel ticket that read:

FOR EMERGENCY COURAGE

"Me? No, it can't be for me, that can't be right!" she spluttered. "I don't want to be brave," she moaned quietly. "Everyone knows I'm not brave enough to be brave."

But there wasn't time to think about that now. Suddenly she heard footsteps coming down the corridor. She'd be in terrible trouble if she was discovered here. She began to feel hot. She began to panic. As she looked at the letters and at Bus Bear, she knew she had to make a decision, and quickly.

So she did.

Grabbing the letters, she frantically looked around the room for somewhere to hide.

"*TAP, TAP, TAP,*" went the footsteps clicking on the corridor linoleum. They were getting closer and closer. She was about to pass out with terror when a sign appeared next to a bucket of mops. It said quite clearly, in big flashing letters:

THIS WAY PLEASE

'What does that mean? Which way?' she thought, looking around frantically. Suddenly a bottom drawer in the filing cabinet slid open. "What?" she spluttered. "That's ridiculous! I won't fit in there!"

The sign changed abruptly:

DON'T BE A CHEEKY MADAM

The footsteps were very close now. Faith looked left. She looked right. It was clear that she had no choice but to do what she was told.

And so, taking a deep breath, she stepped into the drawer. Bus Bear was in one hand, the bundle of letters was in the other. She shut her eyes as tightly as she could.

Chapter 4

Being Brave—Again

"OW! OW! OW! OW! OW! OW!"

Faith sat up and took a look around her. She had sailed headfirst into a springy patch of nettles. Pulling bits of undergrowth from her fuzzy hair, she checked her knees for life-threatening grazes. Where on earth was she? Where were the letters?

Urgently she patted her pockets. Phew! There they were, and Bus Bear too.

Slowly, Faith stood up and looked around, scanning her surroundings. She was in a large green field bordered by hedgerows and oak trees. This was definitely *not* the caretaker's office. In fact, it didn't look like anywhere she knew. Faith had to face facts; she was lost and alone, far from home.

Her eyes began to well up with tears and she sat back down with a despairing thump. "I told you I couldn't do this!" she shouted at the sky. "I'm no good in a crisis!" A munching horse eyed her suspiciously from a far corner of the field. Her stomach started to growl like a grumbling tiger.

'Typical,' she thought. 'Now I'm lost *and* hungry.' Faith felt thoroughly cheesed off.

In spite of her situation, Faith began to think wistfully of school dinners. She had an excellent relationship with Mrs Donna, the school cook, who always let her have seconds of her favourites. Faith loved food. 'Mmmm, Tuesday,' she thought. That meant shepherd's pie with chocolate shortbread for pudding.

She thought about licking the glue on the envelopes but decided against it. What about the nettles? No, she was certainly not desperate enough for those. Feeling around in her pockets, she hoped she might find a stray sweet, but no such luck. All she could find was some fluff and a few biscuit crumbs.

In the distance, she could hear seagulls and the sound of the sea. 'Am I at the seaside?' she wondered. She pondered for a moment. 'I supp-*ose* the seaside might mean nice things, like chips and candy floss.'

She wiped the tears away from her eyes, and her tummy rumbled enthusiastically. The thought of the seaside cheered her up a bit, so she decided to pull her socks up and explore farther afield.

Purposefully she strode across the field towards a five-bar gate, (deliberately not looking at the horse) and climbed over the top.

She let out a little gasp. She didn't know what she had been expecting to find over the top of the field, but now she saw the prettiest seaside town nestled in the hills below. Faith stood looking down on the rainbow-coloured cottages that almost seemed to be tumbling down the valley, like boiled sweets being tipped out of a jar. At the bottom, a yellow sandy beach stretched around the headland and blue water sparkled in the sunlight. Seagulls wheeled and reeled overhead. Boats bobbed like corks and their billowing sails danced cheerfully in the breeze. It looked just the sort of place you might like to go on holiday. She could almost taste the ice cream.

Although now that she looked again, Faith realised that the boats didn't look *quite* like the ones that she was used to seeing on holiday. She strained her eyes and tried to make out the pictures on the sails. "Sort of like... little white faces..." She gulped and took a deep breath. "Oh, dear," she said. Skull and crossbones. That could only mean one thing – pirates!

Immediately Faith dropped down flat into the grass like a frightened rabbit. What now? The town had looked so friendly and inviting a minute ago. Now it was clear that she might get killed, and all before she'd even have the chance to eat any chips...

The bundle of letters in her pocket digging into her ribs interrupted the flow of panic for a moment. It was long enough for her to remember the contents of one of the letters – the one from a pirate. Faith sighed deeply. Not for the first time that day, she had the unpleasant sensation of being in the wrong place at the wrong time. Or, as she was beginning to suspect, the right place at the right time, whether she liked it or not.

"All right, all right," Faith grumbled. "I get it now. I

need to deliver this letter back to its rightful owner. Which probably means being brave. Again."

Sitting up, she took the bundle of letters out of her pocket and thumbed through them. "Ah, here it is." Taking out the piece of parchment, she began to read.

Mrs Blackbeard
34 Castaway Crescent
Felixstowe
BLIGHTY
FE13 QQ

Friday dinnertime

Dear Mummy,

How are you? I'm trying to keep my chin up as you suggested, but life on the open waves is not as much fun as it's cracked up to be. I try to be brave, but sometimes the crew can be a bit unkind and make cruel remarks. They don't mean anything by it, and of course I have to throw them overboard sometimes, but the problem is it's not really my style. Having said that, a good wash does make them smell much nicer.

I am working on becoming terrifying and ruthless like Uncle Bluebeard, but being a savage pirate doesn't come naturally. I know it's an established family firm, but all this 'yo-ho-ho' stuff is a mystery to me. Having said that, where else can you get a managerial post with a wooden leg, an eyepatch and a hook? Not to mention a pet parrot.

I am still very interested in butterflies and am trying to pursue my hobby in secret. Between you and me, I am thinking of branching out into ladybirds, but I don't want to rush into anything.

Thank you for my special ointment; I liked the way you hid it in a barrel of rum. You really are very clever.

Oh, Mummy, I miss our little chats. I long for the day when we can be together again. How is Mrs Bonny's rheumatic knee? And her cats? Send her my love and tell her that green tea can be very beneficial.

Lots of love and hugs,

Blackbeard Jr.

XXXXXXXXXXXXXXXXXXXXXXXXXXXXXXXXXXXXXXXXX

'Hmmm, not very piratey,' Faith thought to herself. She was quite sure that Blackbeard was supposed to be the unholy terror of the seven seas, not a mummy's boy who knew all about herbal teas and ointments. She thought of the boys at school with their playground pirate games full of skulduggery and blood and giggled to herself.

This pirate actually sounded quite sweet. She'd have to help him by making sure nobody ever found out the truth about him – well, other than his mummy, obviously – or he'd never live it down. No one was going to want to play 'Blackbeard the pirate' if they found out he was really a big girl's blouse who loved counting ladybirds more than murdering.

Faith took a deep breath before heaving herself up. It was now or never. She began to walk reluctantly down the steep hill into the village.

Chapter 5

Gloopy Glop and Saucy Pickles

WELCOME TO DOOM VALLEY
Home to the Crazed and Dangerous
(twinned with Felixstowe)

The sign looked as if it had been written in blood. And recently.

Faith gulped and squeezed Bus Bear tightly in her pocket. It certainly didn't sound very inviting. Further up the cobbled lane she could see two little girls playing skipping, which made her feel a bit more relaxed. After all, everybody knows that little girls love to help, so Faith felt sure that they would be able to direct her to Blackbeard's ship.

Exactly one minute later, Faith found herself tied up with a skipping rope, being lowered into a cannon. To be fair, they *were* pirate girls.

"HELP!" she yelled. *"HEEELP!"*

The little girls giggled naughtily, clearly looking around for matches to light the fuse, when luckily a high-pitched shriek came from one of the coloured cottages.

"Griselda! Maud! Lunch is ready!"

A large lady pirate with an enormous bosom appeared in the doorway. She was holding a ladle in one hand and a sword in the other. "Oh, you saucy pickles!" she screeched delightedly. "You've got a little friend! Now untie her and come in or the squid stew will get cold."

The girls wrinkled up their noses and looked thoroughly disappointed.

"Well, all right, bring your friend in too, then. Untie her. No, I *said* untie her first!"

Griselda and Maud reluctantly undid the rope, gripping Faith's wrists tightly with their hot, sticky hands, before marching her into the dark kitchen.

Faith found herself sitting at a wooden table with legs made (alarmingly) out of long white bones.

"So have you been friends with my lovely girls for a while?" asked the big lady, ladling out steaming grey gloopy glop into bowls.

Faith eyed the twins crossly. "No, I wouldn't say that exactly."

The girls grinned, dunking big hunks of bread into the stew.

"It's just that they can get a bit carried away and sometimes accidentally – definitely not on purpose – kill people," said the pirate lady, ruffling the two girls' hair. "The little monkeys," she added affectionately.

Faith was very hungry, and though the squid stew smelt even worse than it looked, she tried a spoonful. To her amazement it tasted delicious, almost as nice as Mrs Donna's shepherd's pie. It made her feel lovely and warm inside and for a minute she almost forgot about all the letters and the task of giving them back she'd got herself into. Cleaning out her bowl, she asked for seconds. The big lady pirate blushed and happily obliged.

After everyone had finished, she gathered up all the bowls and said, "All right, everyone, outside you go to play."

Faith felt gripped with panic. "No!" she squealed.

The big lady pirate looked at her in surprise as Faith tried to pull herself together. "I mean… I'd rather stay in here with you, if you don't mind."

Maud and Griselda glared darkly at her, fingering their skipping rope. Faith edged closer to the safety of their mother's apron.

"Actually, I haven't really got time to play anyway. I've got to find someone." She hesitated. "Someone called Blackbeard."

"Blackbeard!" The big lady dropped her ladle with an almighty clatter. Clamping her hand to her mouth dramatically, she leant on the kitchen table for support. "Oh, no, child. No, no, you cannot mean Blackbeard! Not Blackbeard the Bold. He's bloodthirsty and wicked… the fiercest murderer this side of the sea, and he never… *never* shows mercy. No, child, you don't want to find him. Stay away from him – at all costs – or he'll chop you up into a thousand little pieces and cast you to the four winds for breakfast!"

"But I must find him," Faith protested. "I… I've got something that belongs to him."

"That be as it may, child, and for that reason ye are then

indeed doomed, so ye are, for anyone who has robbed from the most terrible pirate in all history will end up dead as a doorknob."

Faith protested that she hadn't 'robbed' Blackbeard, but it was to no avail. Big lady pirate had worked herself up into a terrible state and was now wringing her apron and pacing up and down the kitchen. "I would no more tell you where Blackbeard is than cut off my own arm. I would no more lead you to Blackbeard than lop off my foot. I would no more…"

She was clearly beyond help. Ignoring her mother's wailing, Griselda leant over to Faith and hissed in her ear, "We'll tell you where he is. Follow us."

And, leading Faith off, the two girls took her through the narrow, cobbled streets, until they were down in the harbour. They stopped outside a house that stood all on its own. Tucked into the higgledy-piggledy wall were small, filthy windows, and above the door a rickety sign that read 'The Drunken Sailor' creaked in the breeze.

"He's in there." Griselda jabbed a finger at the window.

"But I can't go in there. That's a *pub,*" Faith said quickly. They looked mystified.

'Honestly,' she thought despairingly, 'pirates!' Then an important thought occurred to her. She frowned and peered at them. "Why are you helping me anyway?" she asked suspiciously.

"Because this," sniggered Maud, shoving Faith through the open door, "is going to be even more fun than firing you from a cannon!"

Chapter 6

Ladybirds and Achy Knees

Inside, the pub was deafening and smelt really horrible; of smoke and fish and people who were strangers to soap.

'Phew, stinky,' thought Faith, wrinkling up her nose. When she had imagined the pirates in stories, she hadn't realised that just their smell was enough to make you want to run away.

Everyone was guzzling down rum and generally being very loud. None of the pirates seemed to notice Faith as she worked her way through the crowd. How was she supposed to find Blackbeard in amongst all these people?

She needn't have worried. High on the bar stood a tall,

bony pirate, waving a tankard of ale and holding his cutlass aloft. He definitely looked a bit wobbly. "A toast! A toast to the pirate lord!" he bellowed. Everyone fell silent.

"To the cruellest, most bloodthirsty man that ever sailed the high seas!" There was a general chuckle of agreement. "Unstoppable in his quest for gold and adventure! The King of Cruelty, the Master of Murder, the Harvester of Horror – raise your glasses to our captain, the one, the only – BLACKBEARD!"

Everyone cheered and turned to a high table at the back of the room.

There sat Blackbeard, parrot on his shoulder, telescope dangling round his neck. He roared a deep, echoing laugh. "True, true enough! Rum and gunpowder for everyone!"

So, there he was. He certainly didn't look very sweet now. Could the letter *really* be from him?

Faith got closer and crouched down next to the table.

Her eyes were becoming accustomed to the darkness and in the shadows under the table she noticed a delicate china cup painted with scarlet roses. Blackbeard furtively reached down, picked it up for a quick slurp and then put it back on the floor.

Faith crept closer. She sniffed the cup. Tea! She tasted it with her finger. "With lots of milk and sugar!" she giggled to herself. This was definitely her man. Wriggling out backwards, she was about to retreat to a safe distance when a big, hairy hand grabbed her ankle.

Sugarlumps!

"Well, well, what have we here? A little mouse? Or should I say *rat*?"

Everything became deathly silent as Faith found herself dangling upside down, hanging from the steely grip of a giant pirate.

Blackbeard rose to his feet and drove his hook into the table with an almighty thud.

"Gentlemen, it would appear we have a spy in our midst." He gestured to the giant pirate. "Take her to the *Destiny* and throw her into the ship's dungeon." Blackbeard glowered at Faith unpleasantly. "I'll deal with her later."

Faith made the entire journey to the ship upside down, one leg dangling and her hair swinging in her face. Her captor completely ignored her desperate pleas of innocence and did exactly as he had been told, throwing her (most indelicately) into the dungeon.

Faith sat in the darkness amongst the barrels and the chains and felt very alone. She took Bus Bear out of her pocket and pressed him to her face. He smelt of home.

"Oh, Bus Bear," she said in a muffled voice. "What have I done? Why on earth did I decide to return the letters? Am I going to die now? I should have known that I wasn't the right person for the job. Mr Lancelot should have chosen someone else. Probably Jasmine Squire. She'd know what to do. She'd dazzle them with her rising trot."

To her amazement Bus Bear began to get warmer. And warmer. And then even warmer! Actually he was getting too hot to hold… ouch! She dropped him on the floor.

"Sorry about that, BB, but you were burning my fingers!"

She pulled her school jumper over the ends of her hands and bent down to pick him up again. As she gathered him up, she couldn't help noticing that the parcel ticket around his neck had changed. A new message had appeared. Faith read the words out loud:

"WITHOUT FAITH THERE CAN BE NO HOPE"

What? What did that mean? Before she could think about it any more, Faith heard an army of stomping drunken feet clambering onto the ship. They were singing songs (she suspected some were quite rude) and clattering swords.

Stuffing Bus Bear back into her pocket, she was just in time to hear the bolt being slid back on the door. Faith held her breath as the door swung open. There stood Blackbeard, surrounded by pirates, all jostling for position, growling and sniggering.

"So, little girly spy rat, what shall we do with you?" he roared. "Who do you work for? Blood and thunder! If there's one thing as gets me in a rage, it's traitors!"

All the pirates nodded shiftily in agreement.

"Hang her!" shouted one.

"Drown her!" yelled another.

"Make her wash our cheesy socks!" screeched another.

Faith trembled.

"Have you got anything to say for yourself before I make you walk the plank?" bellowed Blackbeard, impatiently tapping his wooden leg on the floor. Faith tried to speak but nothing came out. She felt Bus Bear, hot in her pocket. Silence weighed heavy in the air like treacle.

"Ladybirds!" she finally spluttered. "I work for ladybirds."
Everyone looked very confused.

"And butterflies." She cleared her throat. "I also believe that green tea is very good for achy knees."

Blackbeard stared at her with his one good eye. He stopped growling and grew rather pale. Then he began to chew his fingernail nervously.

The pirates looked at each other in bewilderment.

"Right." He cleared his throat. "Green tea, you say? Ladybirds? Butterflies? Well, I can't say I know as to what you're talking about, no, not at all, I have no interest in these things in any way whatsoever. You are clearly mad as a box of frogs and therefore I feel I should talk to you privately before I kill you horribly."

And with that, Blackbeard turned abruptly on his heel and hastily limped back up the corridor. All the pirates looked extremely disappointed. Sulkily, one grabbed Faith's plait and dragged her up after Blackbeard.

The mighty pirate was now sitting behind his desk in a chair made entirely of human skulls. Faith tried very hard to be brave and stand up straight and hold her head high. She had read about pirate prisoners in her *Big Piratey*

Adventures book and sobbing never got them anywhere. Blackbeard looked up and noticed a couple of scrawny-looking pirates hanging around the door.

"Yes?" He bellowed "What is it?"

"Erm, we thought you might like us to hold her down or we could strangle her for you and we is also very good at stabbin'..."

"GET OUT!" roared Blackbeard furiously. The door slammed shut.

Finally they were alone. Blackbeard's whole body slumped forward like a sack of spuds.

To Faith's horror he started to weep. Faith didn't know what to do so she just patted his arm and said, "There, there now. Erm... don't cry."

Blackbeard looked up through his tears and wailed pathetically, "But you're going to tell *everyone*, aren't you? How do you know about my mummy?" He was stamping his feet under the table. "You're a dastardly rotten girly spy-rat, y'are. How much is it going to cost to keep it a secret?"

"How dare you! I'm not going to tell anyone!" Faith exclaimed crossly. "I'm here to save you."

As she said these words, Bus Bear was like a little fire in her pocket. The heat was like a smile, warming her body. Faith had never saved anybody before and it felt really, really good.

She gave Blackbeard the letter and explained about Mr Lancelot and the ransom note and the strange goings-on in the caretaker's office. When she had finished, Blackbeard looked up at her with tear-filled eyes and gave her a big hug. She found it quite hard to breathe but didn't want to spoil the moment.

"Oh, thank you, thank you! Faith, you really are wonderful," sighed Blackbeard, ruffling her hair, "which is going to make killing you so awkward."

Killing!

It was as if she had had a bucket of iced water thrown over her. "What do you mean, killing?" she exclaimed. "Have you forgotten that I just saved you from losing everything?"

Blackbeard looked a bit irritated. "Well o'course I am most very terrible grateful, but I can't just let you go. That would make everyone suspicious. That would not be good for business."

Faith could see his point, but she definitely did not want to die. "What about all the other letters I have to return?" she said quickly. "Couldn't you just *pretend* to kill me?"

Blackbeard stopped to think for a moment and Faith held her breath, hoping against hope that he would change his mind. Suddenly Blackbeard clapped his hands gleefully and said, "Oh, that would be fun, wouldn't it?"

Faith nodded her head doubtfully.

"Well, you would still have to walk the plank, that's the traditional thing to do," insisted the pirate.

"But isn't that where you tie me up and make me walk off the side of the ship to my certain doom?" pointed out Faith.

Blackbeard crossed the room and opened a large mahogany sideboard. "Yes, that is mostly what happens. Unless, of course, you have..." he turned to face her, "one of *these.*"

In the palm of his hand teetered a tiny glass ball. He held it up to Faith who inspected it closely. It looked like a Christmas tree bauble without a hanger. "This is a Trouble Bubble," explained Blackbeard. "It's the *bubble* that gets yer out of *trouble* – geddit?" The centre of the ball was heaving with waves of coloured light. "I sort of borrowed it in a permanent way," he added sheepishly.

Faith stared at him accusingly.

"All right, I stole it, but they was as dead as a doorknob and didn't need it no more. I *am* a pirate, you know," he said pointedly.

Changing the subject, Blackbeard explained that the Trouble Bubble worked by being an endless source of fresh air underwater. You just popped it into your mouth and pretended to drown; then later, when everyone had gone inside for tea, you simply got out of the water again.

"I've had it for ages," Blackbeard said happily. "I've been saving it for a special occasion, and, by Neptune's beard, I think you're it."

Faith agreed it was a good plan and promised to look terrified in front of all the others.

"You could tremble," said Blackbeard, "and beg for mercy." He leant forward and whispered gleefully, "You could even *wee* yourself a little bit!"

Faith gave him her sternest glare.

"I can see how that might not be the best idea after all," he muttered under his breath, opening the door and ushering Faith out.

The pirate crew cheered with relief when Blackbeard appeared on deck holding Faith at knifepoint. She was doing her best to look frightened and desperate, even rolling her eyes around in a dramatic way and screaming for mercy.

"Don't overdo it," hissed Blackbeard out of the corner of his mouth.

"Found out ye are, ye traitorous mad dog," he bellowed. "It's the long walk into the briny blue for spies, girlies or no, so it is, arrrrrr!"

The pirates roared their approval and waved their swords in the air. Faith was tied up (for the second time that day, she noted wryly) and a blindfold was slipped over her eyes. The Trouble Bubble was wedged safely into the side of her cheek.

'This had better work,' she thought to herself as she was edged along the plank, inch by inch, till finally she could feel the end of the board with her toes.

"Good luck and thank you, little Faith," whispered Blackbeard in her ear, and with that, he shoved her into the wide, blue yonder.

Chapter 7

Turtles and Teashops

The next thing Faith felt was the shock of an ice-cold sea enveloping her small body. Down, down, down she went, softly down to the silent seabed. Faith landed with a gentle thump and sat up. Should she attempt breathing? She tried a tiny whisper of a breath; yes, that was all right. She tried another, bigger one. Yes, that was fine too. The knots on the ropes were tied loosely and she had no trouble wriggling free. Slipping off the blindfold, she was delighted to discover that she was in the most beautiful coral garden.

Faith stood up and took Bus Bear out of her pocket.

"Well, BB, here we are. This is very strange. What do we do now?" He didn't say anything, just stared back blankly with his shiny button eyes. Faith looked up and saw a shaft of light coming from far, far away. She checked her (waterproof) watch. It was probably a bit soon to float up yet. She rolled the Trouble Bubble around until it settled into a comfortable place in the side of her cheek and pondered her situation. 'Maybe we can explore a little first,' she thought.

Knobbly pink trees and fuzzy orange bushes surrounded her. Little fish darted to and fro like busy bees in springtime, and anemones tickled at her shoe buckles. 'What a lovely place!' she thought to herself as a stingray soared by like a flying pancake.

Faith found moving through the water surprisingly easy. Krill trickled past her ankles and her plaits drifted loosely around her shoulders like seaweed as she climbed over a large outcrop of rock.

"This is so much fun, BB," she enthused. "I had no idea that under the sea would be so brilliant!" Faith hadn't had much underwater experience, unless you included an accidental tumble into the shallow end at the local pool.

"It's not even cold! It's not even that wet! It's just so…
so…"

"Yes? What is it? Can I help you?" asked an impatient
voice. A big turtle had sidled up beside her and appeared to
be shuffling leaflets with its flippers. Large letters painted
on its shell said:

TOURIST INFORMATION
YOUR QUESTION IS OUR OPPORTUNITY

The turtle peered at Faith over half-moon spectacles.
"*Yes?* Do you have any questions? Only I'm extremely busy
doing a very important job that I can't really be distracted
from."

It definitely looked like shuffling leaflets to Faith, but
she didn't want to be rude. "I don't think I need any help,
thank you," said Faith politely.

The turtle tutted and sighed. "Honestly, tourists! Barnacle
brains, the lot of them. I suggest you start your tour over
there by the teashop." He grimaced painfully. Faith was
quite alarmed until she realised that the turtle was trying
to smile. "Have a nice day!" the turtle grumbled through
gritted teeth and swam off.

"Teashop? Do they have *tea* under the sea?" Faith looked at her watch again. Come to think of it, it had been a while since Big Pirate Lady's squid stew...

Faith found herself wading towards the entrance enthusiastically. As she got closer, she could see a large piece of driftwood with the name 'Fat Boy Fin's' painted on it. Faith wandered in and sat down at a table made entirely out of limpets.

Immediately a pufferfish with a notepad appeared. She took a very deep breath and blurted: "Good-morning-and-welcome-to-Fat-Boy-Fin's-today-our-special-is-sea-cucumber-sauce-with-periwinkle-pie-followed-by-jellyfish-and-ice-cream-or-sponge-cake-can-I-take-your-order-now?"

"Er, okay," said Faith doubtfully. "That sounds... delicious."

As the waitress sped off, Faith noticed a group of mermaids huddled over a corner table, deep in conversation. Bus Bear began to warm up in her pocket. Wasn't one of the letters from a mermaid?

Before she had time to check, the waitress struggled back with a tray laden with oozy things.

"Here-you-are-madam-the-daily-special-would-you-like-to-sit-with-the-other-mermaids-or…" Faith stood up to help her. "OH-MY-GIDDY-GOLDFISH-YOU'VE-GOT-LEGS!"

The tray dropped with an almighty clatter. This was partly due to the waitress's shock, but also because the limpet table had wandered away of its own accord. The mermaids turned and stared at Faith's legs. She felt herself go bright red as the spotlight of everyone's attention fell on her. The silence was deafening and seemed to go on forever.

A small crab scuttled across the teashop. "Yes? And?" he shouted, waving his claws about in an outraged manner. "So? Not everyone has a tail, you know! Not everyone has to be the flippy-flopping same!"

The waitress tried to shake off the angry little creature snipping at her fins.

"This is leggist behaviour, that's what this is! I could have you sacked for making personal remarks about a crustacean's appearance, because that is *clearly* what she is!" The crab definitely winked. Nobody said anything, but the mermaids squinted doubtfully at Faith's shoes.

"Yes, er, she is certainly a member of the rare mercrab

family," he went on. "Those crabs that have the body of a mermaid but the legs of, er... a crab. And anyway, she's just leaving." With this he grabbed Faith by the ankle sock and briskly marched her (sideways) out of the door.

Chapter 8

Moody Mermaids

"Phew! Thanks! That could have been really awkward," breathed a smiling Faith gratefully.

The crab eyed her pointedly. "Are you being funny?" he said sharply.

('Uh-oh,' thought Faith.)

"Really *awkward*? It could have been a lot worse than that – what if they'd found Marina's postcard in your pocket? What then, Faith the *mercrab*? You seem to have forgotten, Miss Smyth, that you are on a secret mission, not on a '*things I'd like for my tea*' tour!"

"I'm ever so sorry, but who *are* you?" asked a baffled

Faith. "And how do you know about Marina's postcard?"

The crab ignored the question and carried on regardless. "You were even asked *'Do you need any HELP?'* but oh, no, you know best, little Miss Trouble Bubble. *Which,* incidentally, only has one tide-turn left before it runs out and you end up in Davy Jones's locker permanently!"

"But Blackbeard didn't say anything about it running out – he said it was endless!" cried Faith in dismay.

The crab put his pincers on his hips and sighed wearily. "He *is* a pirate, you know. Anyway, we have no more time to waste on shilly-shallying around."

Faith put on her most serious listening face (the one she used with teachers and other people's parents) and tried not to think too much about drowning.

The crab went on. "As I'm sure you are aware, mermaids are beautiful and bewitching and fascinating, with delightful singing voices." He was pacing up and down in an official manner with his pincers behind his back. "What people aren't supposed to know is that they are also a pain in the neck. They are whingers who spend all day gossiping about each other, looking at themselves in mirrors and charting their route to celebrity. Marina is no exception. In fact, she's the worst of the lot. Last year she met a footballer called Alphonse, who promised to marry her, and she's been unbearable ever since."

Faith took the bundle of papers out of her pocket and leafed through them until she found Marina's postcard. She read it aloud:

Alphonse
Seashell Cottage
Penzance
Cornwall

Dear Alphonse,
How are you?
I hope you're having a better time than I am. The weather here is terrible and it rains all the time. You know I am not fond of the damp as it makes my hair frizzy. Every day is a bad hair day and my mascara runs. There is also a distinct smell of fish. Please come and get me this instant.
Yours crossly,
Marina

"Hmmm," said Faith. "I must admit, she's not really what I'd expected; she sounds a bit... annoying."

"Yes, well. It's the same old story," sighed the crab. "Beautiful on the outside but not on the inside." He eyed Faith thoughtfully. "However, there are exceptions to the rule, of course." He gave her a business card. Faith read out the address:

Marina Sargasso
Model / Actress Extraordinaire
4A Titanic Towers
Mermaid Lagoon

"That's where you'll find her, over there," explained the crab, pointing a claw in the direction of a shipwreck sitting in the middle of an underwater lagoon. Faith popped the card in her blazer pocket, right next to Bus Bear.

Except he wasn't there.

"Bus Bear!" She patted her pockets frantically and scanned the ocean floor to see if he had fallen out. "BB!" She called, panic-stricken. "Where are you?"

The crab scuttled up Faith's leg and scrambled into her pocket.

"No! You can't..." started Faith "That's where Bus Bear lives... get out!" She reached into her pocket expecting to feel the hard, knobbly edges of a crab, but instead she felt fur. Definitely fur. "Bus Bear!" she exclaimed delightedly, pulling him out. "Where did you go? And where's that crab gone?" BB's blank eyes stared back at her. A new label was tied around his neck:

NO TIME FOR SHILLY-SHALLYING

The truth slowly dawned on Faith, like an egg being cracked over her head. "Was that *you*, BB? No way!" She gave him a quick squeeze. "Right, no time for shilly-shallying, then, whatever that is. Let's go and find this mermaid and get out of here pronto."

Faith waded towards the bare bones of the shipwreck. As she got closer she could see curtains of seaweed wafting through the portholes. Tethered sea horses delicately nibbled at beautifully manicured lawns of algae.

Faith stepped up to the entrance where a row of shiny doorbells sat next to a speaker phone. She scanned the names up and down, looking for Marina's name. "Pearl

Cockle, Mother of Pearl Cockle, Oceana McMackerel, Anemone Krill… ah, there she is: Marina Sargasso." Faith took a deep breath and pressed the buzzer.

"Yes?" trilled a high voice. Faith could hear pop music in the background. "Who is it? Alphonse, is that you? It's about flippin' time..."

Faith leant in to the speaker phone and cleared her throat. "Erm, no, hello, my name is Faith and I'm here about a letter."

There was a silence and then a sharp, "No, thank you, I would not like to buy dishcloths or miracle cleaning products. Goodbye."

"No, no, I'm not selling anything, I'm here about..." she lowered her voice and hissed, "*a postcard you sent to Alphonse.*"

Another silence, then a grumpy "All right. I s'pose you'd better come up then." The door swished open and Faith stepped inside.

Chapter 9

Thank Goodness for Tourist Information

Faith climbed up four flights of stairs until she came to a door numbered 4A. She was a little out of puff but knocked on the door as enthusiastically as she could. The door opened and she was hurriedly swept inside.

There in front of her was the most beautiful lady she had ever seen. Her flowing hair, which was the colour of bluebells, was threaded with pearls, and her skin was as white as snow. Her eyes were deep, black pools full of stars and her tail shimmered like a rainbow.

Marina looked Faith critically up and down with her hands on her hips. Then she started to slap her tail on the floor impatiently.

"Well, what is it?" she demanded crossly. "Come on, I haven't got all day; I'm getting my scales buffed at five." She looked down her nose at Faith's school uniform.

"It's... erm... it's this... postcard," stammered Faith. She was feeling very nervous and ordinary-looking. "Someone is going to show it to the newspapers and then everyone will know that you're actually very..." She stopped herself just in time.

"Very what?" snapped Marina.

"Very..." Faith struggled to find the right polite words. "*Sensitive?*"

Marina relaxed and shook a mane of hair, which tinkled sweetly. "Well, I do have high standards, I suppose." She fiddled thoughtfully with a little starfish in her hair till it squeaked in pain. "But I can see that not everybody would appreciate that."

Suddenly she sat bolt upright. "But it would mean that I'd be in the papers! Then I'd be famous and I wouldn't need that numbskull idiot Alphonse. All publicity is good publicity, isn't it? This could be the best thing for my career, don't you think?"

Marina turned to look at herself in her hand mirror, fluttered her eyelashes and pouted. "I can see the headlines now: MAGNIFICENT MARINA…"

Faith tutted to herself and put the postcard on the hall table. "Finicky Fishy Fusspot, more like," she whispered to BB. There was no helping some people; beauty really was skin-deep in Marina's case. Dejectedly, she started to tramp down the stairs, just as Bus Bear began to heat up in her pocket. "I know, BB, we did our best."

Faith reached the entrance, but to her surprise she still felt out of puff. 'That's strange,' she thought. 'I'm sure I should only get out of breath going up, not going down.'

Her pocket was getting really, *really* hot now. "Calm down, BB," she said. "It's not the end of the world. Sometimes people can be really disappointing." She fished him out of her blazer pocket. The label around his neck had one word on it in big, red letters:

DROWNING

"WHAT? Oh, no – the Trouble Bubble! Darn that pesky pirate!" Faith began to panic. She tried floating up, but it seemed as if her school shoes were glued to the ocean floor. Suddenly she noticed shapes lurking amongst the rocks; long black shadows, shadows of sharks. "They know, BB," she hissed. "They know it's not working! Oh, Bus Bear, I'm frightened! I need help! What shall I do?"

An impatient voice piped up next to her. "If you had read the sign properly in the first place, then you'd know. '*Your* question is *our* opportunity'."

It was the tourist information turtle! What a relief! He swam between Faith's knees and swept her up onto the back of his shell. Then they swam through the water and into a giant sea cave.

"Aren't we going up to the surface?" asked Faith anxiously.

"Patience, patience," tutted the turtle. "The problem with tourists is they want everything now, now, now."

"Well, as I'm going to drown now, now would be a very good time, actually!" Faith was trying to stay calm, but she was panicky and close to tears.

The turtle was tapping his flippers and looking up expectantly, so Faith followed his gaze.

"What are you looking at?" she asked.

The turtle shushed her as the cave started to tremble –
gently at first, then more determinedly. Water began to
swirl furiously, surging upwards.

"Here it is, right on time," announced the turtle
triumphantly.

"WHAT IS?" Faith was shouting now to be heard over
the deafening roar of the gushing water.

"The Volcano Express, of course," yelled the turtle. "Next
stop, LA!"

"LOS ANGELES?" screeched Faith incredulously.

Abruptly she was sucked up into a vortex of water. Up and
up she soared, whirling and twirling as if she was stuck in the
spin cycle of a washing machine. "AAAARRRGGGHHH!
BB, WHAT'S GOING ONNN?"

But then, as suddenly as it had started, it stopped.
Everything went still and quiet. Faith floated motionless,
suspended as if in a watery dream. There was a *ping*, a lift
door opened and a wall of seawater flowed onto a black
marble floor, carrying Faith along with it. It dumped her
like a drowned cat onto the cold, hard tiles.

Chapter 10

Into the Dragon's Den

Faith spat out the Trouble Bubble. It had a little fuel gauge on it saying 'empty'.

'Phew! That was a little too close for comfort,' thought Faith as she picked strands of seaweed out of her hair. Life was certainly interesting at the moment. She thought about her mum, always encouraging her to be more daring, and, in spite of everything, she smiled to herself.

Where was she this time? It looked like an office building. She knew this because her uncle Brian was an office person. He wore very shiny shoes and an even shinier suit. He was very interested in telephones and different types of takeaway coffee. Now Faith could see that there were escalators, large potted plants and big glass walls around her. She found a bench and sat down. Taking off her socks, she wrung them out and hung them up to dry on the radiator.

By now she was wise enough to realise that she had probably not arrived here by accident. No, the next letter was probably meant for someone in this very building. But who? Who was that going to be? That was when she noticed the leaflets poking out of a rack next to the lift door. She took one and began to read:

Dragonheart Life Coaching
Learn to meet your challenges head-on

She didn't know what 'life coaching' was, but she *did* know that there was a letter from a dragon somewhere in her pocket. She read on:

Do you find life's problems get you down?
Do you wish you were faster, braver or better-looking?

Have you lost your oomph?
With Dragonheart's special help and guidance,
you too can find the hero within.
Email dragonheartdreams@happyheroes.com
or call in on the 28th floor today!

The lift door went *ping* and silently opened. Faith looked around. There was no one else here. The lift was still open and wasn't going anywhere. Clearly this was her ride. She stepped inside. The doors closed and 'Greensleeves' began to play in the background. The lift glided upwards, 1, 2, 3, 4. Up and up, 14, 15, 16. Higher and higher until *ping!* she arrived at floor 28.

She waded out into the softest, deepest red carpet you can possibly imagine. The room was very simple but elegant. Photographs of famous people accompanied by a fierce-looking dragon hung on the walls. There was Queen Victoria sharing a cup of tea, and look! there was Merlin and the dragon doing a thumbs-up sign and grinning madly for the camera. One frame was conspicuously empty. Faith stepped a little closer and squinted at the nameplate.

To Hector,
You rock, man!
Respect,
St George

At the end of the room, a nervous-looking lady in a big, pink pointy hat sat at a glass table. Faith suspected she might be a damsel. "May I help you?" she squeaked.

Faith nodded towards an enormous glossy photograph of a dragon in a very smart suit that was hanging behind the desk. "I'm here to see him," she said.

"Hector?" she replied. "Of course, you must be his four-thirty appointment. Please make yourself comfortable and he will be with you shortly. Help yourself to complimentary mints."

Faith sat down on a big squashy sofa and promptly disappeared down the back of the cushions. She struggled back out again and sat on the arm in what she hoped was a casual manner. Taking a mint from the dish on the coffee table, she sucked it thoughtfully. To her surprise, she felt quite calm. The near-drowning experience and the murderous pirates had put lots of things into perspective.

If she could cope with those, then maybe she was braver than she thought. She took the letters out of her pocket and leafed through them until she found the Dragonheart headed paper. She rattled the mint around her teeth and began to read.

Dragonheart Life Coaching
Director H. Dragon NRHH

Wednesday Lunchtime

Dear George,

Thank you for the signed photograph. I was so pleased to hear that you are feeling more confident these days. Our sessions were clearly helpful. When you first walked into my office, I secretly had my doubts about your dreams of becoming a famous hero, but I did my best to help. As with all my other clients, I hoped to set you on the path to self-belief by talking about your feelings and helping you feel good about who you really are. We even dealt with your strange terror of shrews.

The other day I opened my newspaper and – you'll never guess what – I'm DEAD! Slain by you and your heroic sword, apparently.

'Remarkable,' I thought. I had no idea you were so ambitious. And now you are a saint! Goodness me, you really have been busy.

There is the teeny-weeny problem that I am not dead at all. In fact I'm very alive and this is damaging my reputation. ALL of my clients have cancelled. I went to the bank and they wouldn't let me have any money because... I'M DEAD!

You know as well as I do that you are a big crybaby who couldn't fight his way out of a paper bag! You wouldn't last FIVE MINUTES with me! I'd SNAP you like a twig!

George, you have made me feel CROSS. I do not like feeling cross because then I start KILLING THINGS. This is bad for business. I've eaten FOUR receptionists and it is all your fault for being such a FIBBING WEASEL!

Come for dinner. Bring a big pot. We're going to need it.

Yours hungrily,

Hector x

Faith gulped and nearly choked on her mint.

'Brilliant,' she thought. 'An angry, hungry dragon. Just what I need. So much for feelings of bravery.'

The anxious receptionist tottered into Hector's office with a cup of coffee. The cup was rattling in the saucer. The door closed behind her and two seconds later Faith heard a roar and a scream.

Without a second thought she hastily scribbled 'NOT KNOWN AT THIS ADDRESS' on the envelope, slapped the letter on the desk and legged it back to the lift sharpish.

But the lift door was closed. Sugarlumps!

Frantically, Faith jabbed her fingers at the buttons. She could see the clock on the office wall. Four-thirty exactly. 'Come on, *come on,*' she thought. She could hear footsteps coming from Hector's office. "COME *ON!*" she hissed urgently at the cold steel of the lift door.

Ping. "Phew! About blooming time!" Faith gave a sigh of relief as the door opened, closed and the lift began its descent. 23, 22, 21, down it went. 15, 14, 13, not long now. 9, 8, 7, 6... and then it gave a judder and stopped. Just like that. 'Uh-oh,' thought Faith. 'That is *not* a good sign.'

She pressed some buttons. Nothing happened. She pressed them harder. Still nothing. She tried banging on the door and shouting. No one came. No one could hear her. She sat on the floor for what seemed like an age. At first she felt afraid, then fed up, then afraid again. Ultimately she decided to wallow in self-pity and began to sulk in earnest.

"This is so unfair. I'm doing my best but things keep going wrong and I'm getting really fed up. This is just like when I got stuck in that pothole in Wales."

She pulled BB out of her pocket. "What if I don't want to deliver all of the letters? Why should I? Why can't someone else do it?"

BB had a new ticket around his neck. It said:

WHEN THE GOING GETS TOUGH, THE TOUGH GET GOING

"Well, that's all very well, BB, but I don't appear to be going anywhere, which is exactly the problem, isn't it?"

It was about then that the ringing started. Faith looked around. *Ring-ring, ring-ring.* Noticing a little door in the wall of the lift, she opened it carefully and found a red telephone with a curly wire. Gingerly she picked it up before saying, "Hello?" into the receiver. She could hear tinny music and a woman singing. Faith strained to make out the words on the crackly line:

We have to go on up,
Up together, higher and higher

She recognised the song. It was one of her mum's favourites and she used it in her kick-boxing classes. But why it was coming out of a phone in a lift was a complete mystery to Faith.

She looked at Bus Bear's message and then at the phone.

Slowly it dawned on her. Her gaze crept up to the ceiling, where she could see a trapdoor.

"Oh, yes, very good," Faith chuckled to herself. "Very good indeed."

The trapdoor popped open and a ladder slid down soundlessly. Faith put BB safely back into her pocket and began to climb, one rung at a time.

Chapter 11

Kid Kebab

"Wow!" Faith looked around in amazement. She had come up in a meadow. The grass was lush and green, the sky was blue and birds were singing. Little white flowers peppered the landscape and tufts of sheep's wool adorned the hedgerows like tiny clouds.

Faith climbed up and out of the trapdoor. She dusted herself down, noticing that she had forgotten to collect her socks. Oh, well, at least it was a sunny day. In the distance she could see a note pinned to a gate. She strolled over to have a closer look. It was written very neatly, with lots of swirls and love hearts.

LOST
SIX SHEEP
DON'T KNOW WHERE TO FIND THEM.
LEFT THEM ALONE BUT HAVEN'T COME
HOME.
CASH REWARD
TEXT LBP ON 000986 111

Faith thumbed through the bundle of letters. There was only one person this could be. 'Ah, here it is,' thought Faith. She found a glossy leaflet in the pile and took it out to read.

Li'l Bo Peep's
Sheep Kebab Restaurant

Our takeaways contain the finest ingredients.
Mostly sheep.
(In fact only sheep – very free-range)

Ewe can't bleat our prices!

Call in and buy a takeaway today!

NO VEGETARIAN OPTIONS

10% DISCOUNT WITH THIS LEAFLET

27 Butchers' Row, Rhymington

'Oh, dear,' thought Faith. Little Bo Peep seemed like such a sweet girl in the nursery rhyme. Who'd have thought she would turn out to be such a red-blooded carnivore? Still, she needed to be told about the ransom note. This was definitely best kept out of the papers.

Faith made her way out on to the road and headed down into the town. What was the address? She looked at the leaflet again: 27 Butchers' Row. After half an hour of searching the mazelike streets of Rhymington, she decided to ask for help.

A short, tubby-looking man was sitting on a park bench, so she hurried over. As she got closer she could see that he was wearing a mackintosh and reading a newspaper. "Excuse me, but could you direct me to Butchers' Row, please?"

The man lowered his newspaper and gazed blankly at Faith. His moustache trembled and he appeared very white-faced. Not just pale, he was actually *white*. And woolly. And that moustache was definitely stuck on.

Faith put her hands on her hips. "Are you a sheep?" she said accusingly. He looked petrified. She looked around and couldn't help noticing that all of the people sitting on the park benches were suspiciously woolly-looking too.

"Look," she said, "I won't tell you-know-who, but I do need to find the kebab shop."

The moustachioed sheep looked around furtively and then nodded in the direction of a dark alley on the other side of the road.

"Thanks," said Faith. "And don't worry, your secret's safe with me." And, marching boldly across the road, she headed down the alley.

How could she have missed it before? A hot-pink neon sign was rotating on a roof, casting a sickly light across the gloom of the alley. It flickered on and off. As she got closer she noticed another note pinned to the door, written in the same blue, swirly handwriting that she had seen in the meadow:

Closed until further notice.
Have run out of sheep (again).

Faith knocked on the door until she heard the sound of steps coming down the stairs, the undoing of locks and the sliding of bolts. Finally the door opened a tiny crack.

"What is it?" demanded a tinkly voice.

Faith took a deep breath. "Hello, I'm Faith Smyth and Mr Lancelot has sent me to tell you that one of your leaflets has found its way into the human world. Someone is trying to sell it to the papers, and if that happens, you can say goodbye to your animal-loving reputation. I have come to return it." She handed the leaflet over. Wow, she was getting really good at this. Faith felt rather pleased with herself. BB began to glow in her pocket.

The door opened to reveal a little girl, a bit younger than Faith, with yellow ringlets tied up into bunches with blue satin ribbons. Her cheeks were rosy and she wore a blue dress covered in pink daisies. It had to be Bo Peep.

"Lancelot, you say?" The girl wrinkled up her nose disapprovingly and chewed her fingernail. Then she looked

Faith up and down carefully and gave a wide smile. "Do come in, Faith. How kind of you to help. Would you like some juice? What about a sandwich?"

Faith was starving by now and eagerly accepted. She followed Bo Peep up the stairs and into a kitchen. The little girl stood on tiptoes to reach the apple juice and poured it into a glass. "Will cheese do?" She bustled about making a sandwich. "Only I'm out of... *other things*," she added darkly.

"Yes, I love cheese sandwiches," exclaimed Faith.

Bo Peep placed the sandwiches on the kitchen table and Faith tucked into them wholeheartedly.

"Aren't you eating anything?" asked Faith through a mouthful of bread and cheese.

"No, no, I just love to fatten things up... I mean, see people enjoying their food." Bo Peep had her head in a cupboard full of very large saucepans.

Faith munched happily, but as she did, she could feel Bus Bear getting unbearably hot in her pocket. Whatever did he want now?

"Excuse me, but could I use your bathroom?" asked Faith.

"Sure – it's just upstairs on the right," said Bo Peep. "But don't be long," she added in a sing-song voice, "I've got some lovely cake for *pud*-ding."

'Yum,' thought Faith as she climbed upstairs to the bathroom and locked the door. Quick as a flash, she pulled Bus Bear out of her pocket.

"Right, what is it now, BB? This had better be good. I was having a delicious sandwich with a really nice little girl and you went all hot and bothered. I have to talk to other people, you know; it can't just be you and me all the time. Jealousy is not a pretty thing." As she frowned at him, she couldn't help noticing his label:

GET OUT OF HERE BEFORE YOU BECOME THE FIRST KID KEBAB

"Don't be daft," said Faith dismissively. "Bo's just a little girl."

But it was exactly at this point that the photograph montage on the bathroom wall caught her eye. Could she be seeing things? There was a photo of Bo cooking kebabs on the grill, then another one of her in hunting camouflage gear... oh, and there she was, sharpening her enormous knife collection. Hmm. Maybe BB was onto something after all.

Quick as a flash, Faith climbed up onto the top of the toilet and opened the window. It was a shame about the cake, but she had to get out of there double-quick.

She jumped out of the window and landed – *plop* – in a skip full of fish heads and cabbage. Faith felt a little cross at herself that she'd handed Bo Peep the letter back.

"YIK! YIK! YIK!" She scrambled out and shook all of the fish bits off her uniform. As she strode back out of the alley, she thought it was about time she quizzed Bus Bear.

"OK," she hissed finally, "I think it's about time you and me had a little chat. When I was reading stories to you last night you were just my cuddly bear. But now it seems that you're a lot more than that. A *whole* lot more. You're an important part all of this Lancelot letter weirdness, aren't you? So what exactly is going on? You're hot when I'm in danger and you're hot when I do something good. Or are you just hot when I need to be brave? What does all of this mean, BB? Why me? Why now? This is all so peculiar." Faith sighed a big sigh and turned over the ticket around his neck.

BUT I AM STILL CUDDLY

Faith giggled. "Yes, BB, you are definitely still cuddly."
She gave him a hug as she passed the sheep from before,
reading the newspaper.

"I wonder what sheep like to read about. Knitting?
Dreaming?" she chuckled to herself.

But before she had time to stop and say hello again, a
gust of wind snatched the newspaper out of the sheep's
grasp and blew it down the street. He bleated in panic.

"Don't worry, I'll get it!" piped up Faith, running after
the flapping paper. "Here it is," she shouted. She turned
around to look at the sheep, but he was gone. 'How rude,'
she thought as she looked down at the paper. Staring
straight back at her was the school photo of a little girl,
filling the front page – Faith's school photo, to be precise.

Chapter 12

The Most Speshalist Little Biscuit

The headline read:

LITTLE GIRL MISSING

GINGERBREAD MAN OFFERS REWARD

Gingerbread man? Little girl missing? What exactly was going on?

'I don't even know the Gingerbread Man!' thought a bewildered Faith. 'And I'm hardly missing, anyway – just occasionally lost.' She read on:

"I only popped out for a moment and when I returned, she was gone," reported a tearful Gingerbread Man. "She is so special to me, you see, that I really need to get her back. In her confusion she may also have taken some letters of mine. They don't matter, of course; they mean nothing to me. All I care about is getting my dear, dear, lovely Faith back, safe and sound. If anybody has seen her, please do call the emergency helpline. I shall not rest until I have them... I mean her… back."

The Gingerbread Man had to stop the interview at this point as he was at risk of making himself dangerously soggy with sobbing.

Faith Smyth has a small blue bear with her. Her hair looks as if seagulls have been fighting in it and she is partial to snacks. There have been reported sightings of her in the Doom Valley. One eyewitness has been quoted as saying that she was "Looking for Blackbeard. Probably dead as a doorknob by now. Nothing to do with my girls, though. Squid stew, anyone?"

'What on earth?' thought Faith. She took the remaining letters out of her pocket. They still had a few golden crumbs on them. She thought back to the caretaker's office and the crumbs in the candlelight.

"Of course!" she breathed. "It was HIM all the time! It must have been the Gingerbread Man who wrote the ransom note! But why? He's a fairy tale character too!"

She reached into her pocket for Bus Bear, but he had gone. In his place was a dusty, old diary. On the front, written in very neat capitals, it said:

GINGERBREAD BOY'S
PRIVATE – KEEP OUT, LOSERS!

Faith opened it carefully, unsure of what to expect.

Tuesday 14th Feb

No Valentine's card AGAIN! Loser Lancelot got twenty-four! I was the best runner on sports day by miles but nobody recognises real talent these days. Mr Bickton-Brent droned ON AND ON about it being "bad sportsmanship to tie everyone else's laces together," but what does he know? Mummy and Daddy say I'm the most speshalist little biscuit that was ever baked and they're right. No matter what anyone else says I am NOT short OR crumbly OR spoilt rotten. Ordinary people don't appreciate my magnificence, but one day I SHALL have my revenge. I'll show them who's boss, I'll show them all... (Evil cackle etcetera etcetera.)

G.B. BOY 4 WORLD LEADER
DOWN WITH LOSERS

'Well, that certainly explains a lot. Revenge,' thought Faith, putting the diary back into her pocket. He sounded like a pretty nasty piece of work, that Gingerbread Man. And now, unfortunately, he was a nasty piece of work looking for *her*. Sugarlumps and double sugarlumps. She didn't think he was likely to be the forgiving type either.

She felt a bit scared. He was clearly as mad as a box of gerbils and would probably stop at nothing to get the letters back. Faith hated being in trouble; it made her feel peculiar. She really wanted the feeling to go away.

Maybe she should just hand herself in to the authorities and explain that it had all been a terrible mistake. He might go easy on her if she said that she was very sorry.

She glanced at a news-stand on the other side of the road. The headline read:

BUT YOU'RE *NOT* SORRY, ARE YOU?

What? Faith rubbed her eyes and looked again:

GOVERNMENT RAISES TAXES AGAIN

Maybe she had a disgusting tropical disease and this was all a horrible hallucination or dream. She pinched herself very hard and regretted it almost immediately. "OW!" No, this was definitely real.

And actually, now she came to think of it, she *wasn't* sorry.

"For goodness sake, pull your socks up, Faith," she scolded herself. "He's only made of biscuit mix. Stand up for what you believe in. What he's doing is wrong and horrible, and you jolly well shouldn't put up with it! How dare he think he could expose all the nursery rhymes or stories?" Her pocket began to radiate heat and she felt a rising tide of bravery. "Yes, that's right, BB. Bring it on, gingerboy!

Let's see what you're made of – other than flour, sugar and butter, of course."

The remarkable thing was that Faith actually *meant* it. Suddenly, timid little Faith was a hero for justice! She felt taller, more grown up somehow. Striding confidently into the market square, she held her head high.

A fluffy cat looked up at her, wide-eyed. "Yes, little cat," she said, nodding knowingly, "you are correct. I *am* Faith Smyth, the one in the papers, arch-enemy of the Gingerbread Man." Faith was definitely feeling older and wiser. "Is there anything you would like to say?"

The cat gazed up at Faith dreamily and purred, "You smell like haddock."

Chapter 13

Sherwood Shenanigans

Haddock! What a cheek! Faith sat cross-legged in the park, counting the remaining letters. There weren't many left, but even so – surely it was only a matter of time before the Gingerbread Man caught up with her. She was working against the clock and needed to concentrate hard.

'Which one next?' she pondered as she shuffled through the pile. Her eye came to rest on a scrappy note, made up of hastily stuck together Post-it notes. Faith began to read:

R,

Had to go over to Tuck's as he's got stuck in his rowing machine AGAIN. Can you collect Little Bob from nursery at 4? (Don't forget Bobble Bunny!)

Mary is going to a sleepover at the castle and Guy has archery practice at 5pm (his tights are on the radiator).

Whilst I'm on the subject, could you please stop leaving your arrowheads in your pockets as they cause havoc with the washing. And green things go in the darks wash, not the whites!

Dinner is in the cauldron and just needs heating up.

Hope you had a good day at the office, see you about 6-ish.

Love M x

P.S. Could you check to see if I left the iron on?

It had to be from Maid Marion. And she was a mum! Who'd have thought that she would have gone from brave outlaw to the kitchen-sink queen? Faith felt rather disappointed. She made a mental note never to let this happen to her; she was always going to be a hero from this day forward.

"ARE YOU GETTING IN, THEN, LOVE, OR WHAT?"

Faith nearly jumped out of her skin. Out of nowhere a black taxicab had appeared. The light on the top said VACANT and an enormous sweaty man was squashed into the driver's seat, looking very huffy indeed. "Speaky the English, darlin'? Where-do-you-want-to-go? I haven't got all day, time is money, innit?"

Faith took a deep breath and announced confidently, "Sherwood Forest, please. Maid Marion's house." In her boldest tone she added, "And step on it," before clambering into the back of the cab.

The cab smelt overpoweringly of pine air freshener and kebabs as it trundled off the road and into the woods. The taxi driver turned on the radio. It was the same tinny tune that had played on the lift telephone:

We have to go on up,
Up together, higher and higher

Faith instinctively patted her pockets. Surprise, surprise, BB had disappeared. She looked ahead into the rear-view mirror and scrutinised the driver, who was concentrating hard on the trees. His eyes were black and shiny and his pupils looked distinctly like buttons...

Before she knew it the driver had yanked on the handbrake and the car had come to a screeching halt. He checked his meter and said grumpily, "That'll be twenty quid, love."

Faith perched on the edge of her seat anxiously and leant towards the glass. "Oh, erm… I don't have any *actual* money…"

But the driver wasn't listening. He rummaged in his satchel of change and handed her a twenty-pound note. Tutting to himself, he put away his bag and muttered, "I'll tell you what, this taxi lark is costing me a fortune. The price of cabs these days is disgraceful."

A bemused Faith pushed open the door before stepping into the forest. Squealing away at high speed, the taxi reversed back out of the woods. It did a three-point turn and whizzed away into the distance, leaving Faith standing alone amongst the trees.

'When Lancelot said "Expect the unexpected," he wasn't kidding!' thought Faith. 'What was all *that* about?'

As she ventured farther in she couldn't help noticing a woodland house nestled in a clearing. It looked like a typical fairy tale cottage, except it had a conservatory and a trampoline outside. Walking up to the front door, she gave a polite little knock.

Nobody answered.

There was a bell, so she pressed that, and it played a jangly version of 'Greensleeves'. A dog yapped insanely from behind the glass door. Faith could see it bouncing up and down like a hyperactive frog before a friendly voice piped up: "Hellooo, I'm just round the back!"

As she opened the side gate, Faith spotted a tired-looking lady in an apron, hanging out rows of green pants and socks on a washing line. It had to be Maid Marion. The lady smiled ruefully and put her hands on her hips. She removed a peg from her mouth and said, "Now, if this is about sponsored archery, then you really shouldn't be knocking on strangers' doors."

"No, I'm not here about sponsorship," said Faith, and she explained her situation whilst Marion listened wide-eyed.

"Well," she said when Faith had finished, "you must be exhausted. I imagine you'd like some orange juice and a home-made flapjack? I've got half an hour before I pick the children up from school." They went inside. The house was cosy and welcoming, with lots of family photos all over the walls. Faith picked her way through the sea of scooters and building bricks and they sat down at the big, wooden kitchen table.

"I remember the Gingerbread Boy from school. Nasty, selfish child," said Marion, munching on a flapjack. "When I saw all of that stuff about losing you in the papers, I didn't believe a word of it." She rinsed a baked-bean tin under the tap and threw it over her shoulder into the recycling bin without looking.

She turned around and looked thoughtfully at Faith. "Thank you for your help, Faith. You can't imagine how grateful I am – how grateful, I'm sure, everyone must be."

'That's nice to hear,' thought Faith. There had been a distinct lack of thank yous since the beginning of this bizarre adventure.

Marion continued, "You are a special child, Faith, do you know that?" Her expression changed ever so slightly.

Special? Faith felt a warm glow inside herself. No one had ever called her that before.

But now Marion had turned towards the sink and was beginning to wash up. As she piled the plates on the draining board she said quietly, "You are also terribly young to have taken on such a task. I feel concerned for you, so far away from your family."

Faith gulped, feeling her new-found bravado sag. Now that Marion had pointed it out, she felt overwhelmed by homesickness. Even if her parents and brother and sister weren't always the kindest to her, the cosiness of the kitchen and the smell of washing powder made her eyes well up with tears. Marion's children were very lucky.

In a very small voice, Faith said, "Do you think I could have a hug, please? Only it's just that sometimes it gets a bit lonely being a hero."

Marion wrapped her arms around Faith and gave her a comforting squeeze.

"But you're not alone, Faith," she said, smiling. "What about this character?" And she produced BB out of Faith's pocket, like a rabbit out of a hat.

Faith wiped her eyes and grinned at BB. "So you're back, then?" She looked up at Marion. "It's time we were off, but thank you for..." She looked down at her shoes sheepishly. "Well, thank you for being so nice."

"And thank you for giving me my letter back." Maid Marion gave a low, sweeping bow. She was just showing

Faith to the front door when suddenly she remembered something. "Oh, and don't forget these!" Dashing over to the washing pile, she picked up a pair of freshly washed white socks.

"My socks! But *how* did you…?" stammered Faith, "*When* did you…?" Marion winked and waved goodbye.

As Faith walked away she began to understand that heroes come in many different shapes and sizes, and that sometimes you find them in the unlikeliest of settings...

★★★★★

Faith followed the woodland path for some time until dusk began to fall on the forest. Owls hooted and bats swooped around her head. She smiled wistfully to herself when she remembered explaining the 'scary bat' dream to her dad over a milkshake. Being at home all seemed such a long time ago; just how long *had* it been?

She began to yawn. It was a struggle to keep her eyes open. She came to a fallen tree trunk covered in moss and lay down next to it. Somewhere in the distance she could hear the sound of a river, crooning its bubbly lullaby. 'Just a little rest,' she promised herself, just a resting of her eyes for five minutes. The leaves were squashy and soft, just like a mattress. Wood pigeons cooed as ripples of sleep flowed over her thoughts, lulling her into oblivion...

When she awoke it was still dark; the moonlight filtered through the trees, casting long blue shadows across the forest floor. She could feel something in her mouth, something like string or dental floss. Yes, it was knotted around her tooth! What on earth...?

Her eye followed the string out of her mouth, up into an old oak tree. She squinted and could just make out a tiny figure balancing a teetering rock on one of the branches, a rock that was attached to Faith's tooth by a piece of dental floss.

"NOOOO!" she shouted, but it was too late; the little person pushed the rock off anyway. "OW!" yelled Faith, as the floss snapped clean in two and the rock crashed to the ground below.

"DRAT AND DOUBLE DRAT!" complained a small voice.

"How DARE you?" demanded Faith furiously, clutching her face and marching towards the tree at great speed. She jabbed an accusing finger at the little person in the tree. "What is your problem? You could have pulled my tooth out!"

The tiny lady retorted with a weary sigh, "Not likely with my current run of luck."

"Do you mean to say that you were actually *trying* to steal my tooth?" Faith was outraged. "What a sugarlumping nerve!"

The little person slid down the trunk of the tree with impressive speed and agility. "Desperate times call for desperate measures, OK?"

Was that an East End accent?

Faith began to calm down a little. She inspected the thief more closely. "Are you a fairy?" she asked, her curiosity gradually getting the better of her.

The tiny person jabbed a bony finger at Faith and said, "Not just any old ordinary fairy, if you don't mind." She cleared her throat and added seriously, "I'm a professional."

The fairy deftly scaled a nearby tree stump, struck a noble pose and held out her hand. "I should introduce myself. I'm Floss Daly – otherwise known as the Tooth Fairy."

Chapter 14

The Tooth, the Whole Tooth and Nothing but the Tooth

In spite of being rather impressed by the fairy in front of her, Faith pretended not to be. "You're not supposed to steal teeth that are still being used!" she cried out. "That would make you nothing more than a common thief!"

The Tooth Fairy looked shamefacedly at her boots, kicking her heels against the moss. "Yeah, well, whatever. I'm not normally like this, y'know. I've been driven to it. Times are hard and I need all the work I can get at the moment."

"What do you mean?" asked Faith.

The fairy looked very serious, leaned forward and

whispered secretively, "The tax man's after me stash of cash. I've got a humongous bill to pay."

Faith had heard of tax. It was when grown-ups had to give some of their wages to the government to pay for schools and hospitals and roads. Faith imagined it all being saved in a great big penny jar. She had always thought it sounded like a very sensible idea because those things were for everybody to share. But for some reason adults always got very huffy about it. Whenever her dad got a tax demand he would sulk for days and days and had to drink lots of wine until he felt better.

Faith was just pondering this new information when the Tooth Fairy said matter-of-factly, "So I'll be needing that letter back now."

Letter! How did the Tooth Fairy know about that? Faith stared disbelievingly, her mouth flapping like a fish. "How do you know about the letters?"

"Saw it on the telly," the Tooth Fairy said, scratching her head. "Gingerbread Man's come clean and confessed that you're a ROBBER. Everyone knows wot you got. He says that you've got to be stopped before you sell the letters to the papers. So you gets what you deserve, if you ask me.

You've got a nerve an' all, calling me a thief! You're the one everyone's looking for. You're public enemy number one, you are."

What a weasel that gingery biscuit was.

"Me? That is so not fair!" cried Faith. "I'm no thief. I've just been trying to help by returning the letters to their rightful owners. It was the Gingerbread Man who was the thief, and a liar as well!" Faith had gone beetroot red and felt very hot indeed. "I'm just trying to be heroic. I've had to learn to be brave and be good in a crisis, and lots of other things that do not come naturally to me either!" She should have seen this coming. She should have known that the Gingerbread Man wouldn't play fair.

"Listen, what you do in your spare time is none of my business," the Tooth Fairy said, "but one thing's for sure – I need that letter back." She held out her hand. "Come on, chop chop!"

Faith took the letters out straight away. She couldn't wait to hand the Tooth Fairy's over – after all, that was what she was here for. Here it was – the small brown envelope addressed to 'Investigations, The Tax Office'.

She looked suspiciously at Floss. "How do I know you

can be trusted?"

The fairy rolled her eyes and sighed. "Fine, read it for yourself."

Faith opened it up and began to read.

THE TOOTH, THE WHOLE TOOTH AND
NOTHING BUT THE TOOTH
THE TOOTH FAIRY LTD
SERVING THE PUBLIC SINCE ONCE UPON A TIME

Mr Smythe-Robinson

Investigations

Inland Revenue

27-98 Gumtree Rd

London W1

Dear Mr Tax-inspectory Man,

Thank you for the whopping bill. It is indeed unfortunate that I don't seem to have paid as much tax as I should have. I understand that you are upset. If I was a silly Tooth Fairy I would say, "Calm down, Mr Tax Man, or you'll give yourself a nasty headache." But I'm not a silly Tooth Fairy and I can explain everything.

The Tooth Fairy Ltd is a small family business that consists of only me. Yes, I do handle a lot of cash but I've got loads of bills to pay too. For example, my insurance costs have gone up as they now say my job is 'high risk', and they have put in a squashability clause. Travel expenses are sky-high and the equipment costs a blooming fortune (see attached receipt). And by the way, going to the gym is not a 'hobby'. Teeth are heavy and it's important that I stay in tip-top condition.

I'd be the first to admit that I'm not great with money – I tend to splash it about. It might also surprise you to learn that I can be a bit messy. I'd like a secretary but fairies aren't known for their organising skills. Anybody else's bottom would be too big for the chairs. (Tee-hee!)

I'm throwing myself on your mercy, Mr Man. My heart's in the right place (even if the money isn't). And I'm dead sorry about the bad spell I put on you the last time we met. I hope the swelling has gone down and your teeth fit back in your head.

Yours faithfully,

The Tooth Fairy

"See? Now can I have the letter back?" The Tooth Fairy eyed Faith anxiously. "Listen," she sighed impatiently, looking Faith straight in the eye, "if children think that I'm short of money, they'll start worrying. Next thing you know they'll stop believing in me, and that, let me tell you, is a sticky end for any mythical character."

She was right, of course. Faith stared levelly at the fairy and said, "I was always going to give you the letter. That's what I'm here for. The only reason I'm stuck in this wacky world is to give back the letters! It's the whole point, no matter what that jumped-up dog biscuit says." She handed Floss the letter.

Carefully folding the two remaining letters, she put them back in her pocket. As she did so, she felt the crispness of folded paper nudge against her fingertips. Of course! The twenty-pound note given to her by the taxi driver! That was a start.

"Would this help to pay your tax bill?" she asked excitedly, whipping the note out and waving it in the air.

The Tooth Fairy clapped her little hands gleefully and did a little dance. "I should cocoa!" she squealed, grinning and showing off an impressive set of gnashers. "Wow!

Thanks, little girl!" She popped the money in her wallet before slapping it shut. The rosy glow of the rising sun was changing the colours of the woodland from blue-black to a golden peach. She glanced at her watch. "Oops! Gotta go; I'm more of a night worker really."

As the Tooth Fairy went to leave, she hesitated for a moment, turning her gaze to Faith in the morning sunlight. "The Gingerbread Man wasn't joking about your hairdo, but for the record I don't reckon he was tellin' the truth about the other stuff. Sorry about the... y'know... tooth thing. Anyway, you'll find the Big Bad Wolf down in the valley."

Faith checked the remaining letters before looking up, shocked. "How did you know he was next? I deliberately tried to keep the names hidden. It's *supposed* to be confidential."

The fairy grinned a big toothy grin. "I told you; I'm a professional. It's my job to notice the little things."

And with that she leapt on to the forest floor, broke into a high-speed sprint and vanished before you could say 'fluoride'.

Faith giggled to herself. "What a funny little person, BB, don't you think?"

She went to pull the bear out of her pocket but he was gone again. Faith tutted; this was becoming a habit. In his place was a bundle of papers. She read the title page:

Little Red Riding Hood
Screenplay by Grimm Bros. Ltd
Big Bad Wolf's PRIVATE copy

It was a script. This was interesting; Faith liked a good story. She was about to settle down to a nice, cosy read when she noticed out of the corner of her eye that a set of traffic lights had mysteriously appeared. No, it was a pedestrian crossing. Faith looked for a road or some traffic, but there was nothing but the sound of rustling leaves and birdsong.

A family of rabbits hopped up to the crossing and nervously pressed the button. After a minute, the sign changed from 'DON'T HOP' to 'HOP'. The furry family made a frantic dash to the other side.

'How odd,' thought Faith with amusement.

It was then that a white limousine with blacked-out windows suddenly appeared out of nowhere, careering around the trees at high speed. It roared past Faith, nearly knocking her down.

"Hey!" she yelled. "Watch where you're going!"

It disappeared down the hill in a cloud of dust, but not before Faith spotted the number plate:

RED ROOLZ

Well, no prizes for guessing who that belonged to. Clearly Little Red Riding Hood was doing quite well for herself these days.

'Into the valley it is,' Faith thought to herself. 'Follow that limo!'

Chapter 15

Theatrical Thunderpants

Faith stood on the crest of the steep-sided gully, watching the army of people below. There were all sorts of film types milling about – sound technicians balanced big fluffy microphones on tree branches, and the director watched scenes on a little television screen. Cameramen sat drinking coffee out of paper cups while a lady in a puffer jacket walked about holding a clipboard and barking orders.

At one end of the valley there was a huddle of caravans, one noticeably larger than the rest. 'BIG RED' was emblazoned down the side in impressive scarlet letters. Faith noted the white limo parked outside.

The other caravans were nowhere near as grand. One of them looked as if it had been rescued from a skip. In fact it might even have *been* a skip. Dangling from its door handle was a tatty cardboard sign. It was handwritten in black felt-tip pen and simply said, 'The Big Bad Wolf'.

'Oh, dear,' thought Faith. 'How un-showbiz.'

She scanned the valley, looking for the Wolf. She felt a little bit scared, if the truth be told. The Big Bad Wolf used to give her bad dreams, with his enormous eyes and sharp fangs. After her near miss with the dragon she naturally felt a bit anxious.

Suddenly she spotted two figures sitting next to a tea trolley. One was unmistakably Little Red Riding Hood. She had sunglasses on and was clutching a little pink dog under her arm. Make-up artists fussed around her with brushes and powder puffs. By contrast the mangy figure sitting next to her was scowling in his chair, peering through half-moon spectacles and hunching over a book.

Faith tried to get a closer look. She screwed up her eyes and squinted, but it was no good. 'Hang on a moment,' she thought, reaching into her pocket. Out came a pair of binoculars. 'I'm getting rather good at this,' she thought cheerfully.

Holding them up to her eyes, she looked at the book cover. The title came into focus: *Delicious Vegan Dinners for the Single Man*. Faith was intrigued. Time to read that letter.

Lionel Darling Management

34 Windmill Lane

Truro

Cornwall

TR14 7NW

Sunday lunchtime

My Dearest Lionel,

How are you? I am fine, except for the continuing drama in my digestive system. Quite frankly I suffer with dreadful wind. The doctor says it's a result of stress, but I know I haven't been the same since I ate my first grandma. I am now fully vegan as dairy and eggs have the most terrible consequences. As do lemons and nuts. And sugar. And Cheesy Puff-puffs. Truly, I'm only half the beast I was.

I must admit to feeling a little under pressure and I'm not getting on with the others. The woodcutter calls me 'The Big Bad Bottom Burp' and the pig actors (who aren't even in the cast) hang around the set and chant, "I'll huff and I'll guff until I blast my pants off." It's all so childish. Only the other day that girl (you know to whom I am referring) gave me a shove and I fell into a bush. The only consolation was that she was laughing so much she choked on her stupid cake. She could do with an exclusion diet or seven.

I feel the time has come for me to move on. These people are twits and I'm fed up with being a baddie all the time. As I think I may have mentioned before, I feel much more suited to the romantic lead.

Remember the glory days, Lionel? The summer season in Stratford when I made all the ladies swoon with my booming Hamlet? Ah, the adoration, the autographs... As you know, my large eyes and sharp teeth have often been remarked upon. My talent is wasted here. I'm willing to try anything – even panto – as long as there are no children. Or little pigs. Is your agent's fee still a very competitive 42%?

As Shakespeare said, all the world's a stage, and I am its humble servant, a strolling minstrel, a mere master of my worthy craft.

Must dash; last night's curry is taking its toll,

Yours faithfully,

The Big Bad Wolf

Tears of laughter streamed down Faith's face as she put the letter back in her pocket. She knew she shouldn't, but she just couldn't help herself. Who'd have thought that the Big Bad Wolf would turn out to be a Nice Old Wolf?

Faith tried to imagine him as a romantic leading man. She tried and tried but she just couldn't see it working. That matted, grizzled fur and the knitted cardigan would look more at home at a jumble sale. "Poor old thing," she giggled to herself.

She put the binoculars away in her blazer pocket and began to climb down the hill, skirting the edges of the gully and scrambling between the trees.

Finally she reached the bottom of the valley and crept behind the caravans.

She let herself into the Wolf's caravan. This wasn't particularly difficult as the door was tied shut with an old sock.

She cast her eye about the dingy room, her eyes adjusting to the low light. There was a framed picture of William Shakespeare hanging over the mantelpiece, and dotted around were sweet little pictures of kittens and lambs. She had to admit, the caravan did smell a bit... cabbagey.

Bookshelves lined the walls, groaning under the weight of old, dusty scripts. Faith took one down: *A Midsummer Night's Dream, 1595.*

As she opened it a faded, pressed rose fluttered onto the threadbare rug, followed by a miniature portrait in a gilded frame. Faith picked them up carefully and looked at the picture.

It was a portrait of the Wolf, but he was neither big nor bad. Instead he was young and handsome and dressed in a velvet theatrical costume. His fur was glossy and his teeth were dazzlingly white. He was on one knee, gazing meaningfully at a skull. On the back there was a message in elaborate handwriting:

To the magnificent, majestic Wolf,
What a magical performance. One has never felt so moved.
Your Hamlet was a triumph.
Kisses,
Queen Elizabeth the First

Faith didn't feel like laughing any more. She felt ashamed. Poor old Wolf, he'd been right all along. He had been one of the greats.

Carefully, Faith put the script and its contents back on the shelf. Then she reached into her pocket and pulled out a packet of anti-diarrhoea medicine, which she placed on the table along with the letter.

"Are you looking for an autograph?" boomed a deep voice accusingly.

Faith looked up to see the Wolf staring at her through the grimy window, his annoyed face pressed up to the glass. She felt sick. This wasn't supposed to happen. "Because if you are," he went on, "you should ask politely rather than rifling through my personal things."

'I could run, or scream or kick,' thought Faith, but really she doubted that any of those things would be useful, seeing as she was rooted to the floor in terror. Where was Bus Bear when she needed him? She opened her mouth to offer an explanation but no sound came out except for a tiny squeak of panic. Faith could feel the bit behind her knees beginning to sweat.

"Hang on a moment – I know you!" The Wolf's eyes expanded to the size of saucers as he put his paw up to his mouth. "You're... you're that ruthless letter thief from the papers, the 'Merciless Magical Mail Marauder'! Oh my stars and buttons! Odds bodkins! They said you shouldn't be approached at any price. Please don't hurt me, I beg of you. I'll do anything you say!"

Well, *this* was a turn-up for the books. Faith hadn't imagined her criminal reputation could be a good thing. 'Merciless Magical Mail Marauder' had a nice ring to it too, even if it was a bit of a mouthful.

Quickly recovering her composure, Faith did her best to speak in a menacing tone. She cleared her throat with a little cough. "All right, come in here and sit down – but no funny business, mind. I'm watching your every move."

The Wolf edged in through the door and nervously perched on a beanbag. His huge body seemed to fill the whole caravan. His eyes fell on the letter on the table. "Oh, my goodness," he whimpered tearfully, "that explains why Lionel hasn't been in touch. I was beginning to think he was avoiding me."

Quivering, he looked up. "What do you want?" He hid behind his enormous forearm. "Please don't hurt my face! Just leave me alone."

It was sad really. Faith was stumped as to what to do next. Then, in a flash, she saw an opportunity to do something good. Taking a deep breath, she put her hands on her hips sternly and said, "I want... I want you to believe in yourself. I have it on good authority that you are a very fine actor. You should be proud of who you are and... and *sparkle*, just like that power-crazed madam out there. Brush your fur and throw away that terrible cardigan; it's disguising the magnificent beast that you are."

The Wolf didn't say anything for a moment. He fingered his cardigan sulkily and pouted. "But I like my cardigan," he said sullenly. "I bought it on a day trip to Cardiff in nineteen fifty-two."

"And it looks like it!" retorted Faith. "You need to take better care of yourself if you're going to be the actor that you were. I'm sure that would help your embarrassing tummy problems to settle down as well."

The Wolf began to relax. He crossed his legs and sat back. "I hope you don't mind me mentioning this, luvvie, but this isn't really typical of a criminal assault. I think you're supposed to rob me or shoot me or something dreadful. Not boost my morale and give me style tips."

Faith sighed and flopped down on another beanbag. A cloud of dust flew up in the air. "That's because I'm not a criminal," she sighed. "I'm just a little girl."

Over a cup of peppermint tea and a dairy-free biscuit she explained the whole story.

The Wolf listened intently. When she had finished, he got up and began to scan the bookshelves.

"What are you doing?" asked Faith curiously.

"It's just that I'm sure I've heard this one before," he muttered absent-mindedly, concentrating on the titles, tracing his paw along the spines. "Ah, I knew it!" he announced triumphantly. "I never forget a story. Here it is."

He took down a red, leather-bound script from the top shelf and blew a thick layer of dust off it. It was tied with crimson ribbons, and in gold embossed letters on the front it said:

Magical Mail
by F. Smyth

Faith had a funny feeling. It was if she was watching herself in slow motion from a distance. Her mouth opened and shut, but no sound came out. 'This is impossible,' she thought. 'This is absurd.'

The Wolf gently handed her the book and she turned the pages one by one. Ridiculous or not, it was her story, typed neatly in black ink.

It began with her loneliness (how strange that she should have forgotten that already). There was the caretaker's office and BB, Blackbeard and Marina, Hector the scary dragon and Bo Peep, the Gingerbread Man, Maid Marion, the Tooth Fairy and now the Big Bad Wolf. The last few pages were empty, though.

Shutting the book carefully, she said, "My story hasn't quite finished yet, has it?"

"No, old girl, it looks as though it hasn't," replied the Wolf gently.

Faith looked up at him in the gloom of the caravan. "Wolf," she asked hesitantly, "is it a 'happily ever after' sort of story, do you know? Or is it one of those... sad ones that don't end so well?"

The Wolf took her little hand in his giant paw. "No one can know. When you are writing your own story, the ending is always a mystery."

Faith didn't feel particularly reassured by this piece of

wisdom. "How do I know what to do next, though?" she asked him.

The Wolf suddenly stood up, as if a thought had occurred to him. Looking dramatically into the middle distance, he struck a noble pose and boomed, "To be, or not to be, that is the question. Whether it is nobler in the mind to face the slings and arrows of outrageous fortune..."

Shakespeare. It was no good, he was off.

Faith opened the script and read the last line for herself:

As the Gingerbread Man crept towards the caravan he could see Faith through the grime of the window, reading a red book.

The Gingerbread Man! Help!

Chapter 16

When Cookies Go Crackers

Faith dropped to the floor like a stone. Sugarlumps, sugarlumps, sugarlumps! She had only one letter left and she would be darned if the Gingerbread Man was going to stop her now.

As Faith lay spreadeagled on the dusty old carpet, she couldn't help noticing a cardboard box marked 'Props' wedged under the table.

Crawling over to it, she pulled out the contents: bricks, straw, sticks and three pig costumes. 'Wow,' she thought, 'those pigs certainly were little.'

Quickly she picked out the biggest outfit and wriggled

into it. OK, so it smelt slightly of ham and was a bit tight, but it would have to do. Disguise complete, but how to get out?

The Wolf was still ranting on and on dramatically, striding up and down the length of the caravan, completely unaware of Faith's predicament and her change of outfit. As he paced, his claws rucked up the corners of the rug, revealing a big hole where the bottom of the caravan had rusted away. Thank heavens for that.

Urgently, Faith squashed herself through the hole, sliding soundlessly into the thick, lush grass beneath the caravan. Hardly daring to breathe, she lay as flat as a pancake amongst the dandelions. Just at that moment, she heard a knock on the door. Then it opened and shut above her. The Wolf had stopped pacing now and she could hear two muffled voices arguing in heated tones.

This was her chance! She rolled out from underneath the caravan and ran as fast as she could (which is no mean feat in a pig costume). Dashing along the bottom of the valley, she ran straight through the film set. They were filming the scene where Little Red Riding Hood skips innocently through the woods.

"CUT!" yelled a furious director as Faith tore through the set. "WHO THINKS THIS IS A PIG MOVIE? THAT'S NEXT WEEK, YOU NUMBSKULLS! I SAID *CUT*!"

Faith just kept on running, sending chairs and coffee cups flying. Finally she reached the top of the valley and hid behind an old oak tree. Gasping for breath, she slumped to the ground, her heart thumping. Was she scared? Maybe. Although she had a sneaking suspicion that she was more thrilled than frightened. She couldn't decide whether she wanted to laugh or cry.

She didn't have long to decide, for there, already halfway up the slope, was the Gingerbread Man, and boy, did he look *angry*. Faith tore off the pig costume and hurled it down the valley. She took flight again, running as fast as her legs would carry her.

As she galloped through the bracken, Faith knew that it wouldn't be long before the Gingerbread Man caught up with her (running was his speciality, after all). She needed to think quickly.

'Water!' she thought. 'Of course! The Gingerbread Man hates water! I need to find a river, and fast.'

In a flash, she remembered the watery lullaby that had

sung her to sleep in the woods. The Gingerbread Man was hot on her heels. She scrambled over moss-covered rocks, through woodland and down to the pebbly shores of a shallow river. Throwing herself into the icy cold water, she splashed droplets everywhere before wading breathlessly across to the other side.

Faith collapsed onto the shore victorious; she had outwitted her enemy. There was no way he could get across without turning to gingery mush.

Faith's arch-enemy stood wordlessly on the other side, his currant eyes glittering dangerously. He scanned the river up and down and stamped his little toast-coloured feet angrily. Triumphant, Faith grinned and shouted cheerfully, "Never mind, better luck next time, eh?"

It was then that he took out the cling film.

To Faith's horror he peeled off a sheet and wrapped himself in it from head to toe. Did this biscuit never give up? He waded into the shallows and began to do a front crawl at top speed.

'Uh-oh,' thought Faith. 'Time for Plan B.' Only she wasn't exactly sure what Plan B was. She was pretty sure that it was going to involve running, so that's exactly what she did. She ran and she ran as if her life depended on it. She ran up hills and over fields, she ran down lanes and up a mountain. She ran so far that eventually she ran out of land. Breathless and jelly-kneed, an exhausted Faith teetered on the edge of a ravine. She had nowhere else to go. Below her lay a jagged rocky canyon. The Gingerbread Man had finally caught up with her. He staggered towards her breathlessly.

"Give-me-the-letter," he gasped.

This was the first time Faith had heard him speak. His voice was extraordinarily high and wobbly, like a toddler about to explode. As drained and exhausted as she was, she began to giggle.

"That is the silliest voice I've ever heard! How can you be an evil genius if you sound as if you've got a squeaker stuck in your windpipe?" Faith slapped her thighs and laughed until tears rolled down her cheeks.

The Gingerbread Man stood motionless and silent while Faith rolled around on the floor hysterically. He was clearly not amused. Finally she wiped her eyes and pulled herself together. She sighed deeply, looked him straight in the currants and said, "You are a silly little man. You have done a very bad thing, and if you think I'm going to give you the last letter then you are bonkers. That is the last thing I'm going to do."

"Oh, well," he squeaked, "you won't be wanting this, then, will you?"

He held up his gingery hand. In it was Bus Bear. Faith felt the blood drain down to her shoes. How had he got BB? Maybe he had fallen out of her pocket when she was running, or maybe even at the caravan. She'd been concentrating so hard on the chase that she hadn't checked him for ages. 'Stupid, stupid girl,' she thought. She felt like kicking herself.

"Give him back, you gingery weasel, give him back now, or I'll... I'll..." Faith felt scared and furious at the same time.

"Or you'll what, girlie-girl?" He was looking very smug. "*Give him back now,*" mocked the Gingerbread Man in a sing-song voice. "Not so smarty-pants now are you, little Miss Goody Two-shoes? I've been watching you and your stupid bear, and I've been looking forward to teaching you both a lesson."

He was really ranting now and working himself in to a

lather. "How DARE you steal my letters? They were going to be my passport to an easy life. As if people believe in fairy tales these days anyway! Those losers deserved everything they were going to get, but you had to interfere! What kind of hero are you, anyway?" He pressed his palms together as if begging for mercy and rolled his eyes up to the sky. "*Oh, BB, I'm so lonely; oh, BB, what shall I do?* Lancelot must have been off his rocker to choose a wimp like you. As if someone like you would stand a chance against someone like me. Useless, whiny, crybaby Faith. No wonder you haven't got any FRIENDS!"

At this, Faith felt herself go hot with embarrassment, and a fiery rage swept through her. "Fine, come and get your stupid letter if it's so important!" she cried. Faith thrust the neatly folded letter out towards him. "Just give me my bear back."

The Gingerbread Man flung BB aside carelessly before lunging at the letter. Moving with lightning speed, Faith took a step towards the top of the ravine and dropped it over the edge.

"NOOOO!" screeched a hysterical Gingerbread Man. Frantically he dived after it, tumbling thousands of feet down into the gully below before hitting the bottom and disappearing in a cloud of crumbs. *Poof!*

Faith breathed a sigh of relief as she picked up BB and stood on the cliff edge, peering down over the rocks. Leaning over the edge she shouted cheerily, "See ya, wouldn't wanna be ya!"

She held up BB, dusted him off and looked him straight in his shiny button eyes.

"And that, my dear bear," she said calmly, "is how the cookie crumbles. Now, where's that letter?" She fumbled in her pockets. "Ah, here it is. Honestly, as if I was going to give that jumped-up cracker the last letter." BB looked at her quizzically. "Well, I'm not a fool, BB. I gave him one of the dragon's life coaching leaflets. He was just too desperate to notice, that's all.

"Now, where to next...?" Faith whipped out the last letter and looked at the return address:

Olga D'spicable,
Shangri-La Health and Beauty Spa,
Lake Geneva,
Switzerland

She cleared her throat and read the letter out loud.

(Uncle) Olaf the Despicable
Dunromin Rest Home
Misery Island
The Sea of Black Despair
North Wales
MI23 7ZG

Tuesday lunchtime

Darling, darling Uncle Olaf,
  What can I say? I have undergone a life-changing experience. I have finally discovered the real me, found my inner beauty, located my peaceful, lovely self.
  "How have you done this, Olga?" I hear you ask.
  Why, through the shopping channel and daytime TV, I reply! Hours and hours of shopping and watching, watching and shopping. In between times I have beauty treatments and drink smoothies made of pink goo.
  Here at Shangri-La, life is beautiful. I am in an ocean of calm; a lake of love. As you know, I had been going

130

through a bad patch. The gingerbread house plan didn't turn out as expected and resulted in some serious burns on my part. The doctors have stressed that I mustn't spend any more time in ovens or in the company of angry children. I was sent here to recover and it has transformed my life.

Apparently in order to BE good, you must first LOOK good. I realised that I had let things slide a little in the looks department (no, no, really, it's true) and I got to work on improving myself straight away.

It occurred to me that eating children might be bad for the waistline, so I made a solemn vow to eat jelly babies and alphabetti-spaghetti ONLY. I have bought myself a tummy-toning hula hoop and a simply stunning pair of dangly earrings made out of 100% pure plastic. I am one hot babe.

As if this were not enough, I have decided to abandon my old, evil ways and open a hairdressing salon called 'Krazy Kutz'.

Got to dash — I'm having my nails done at 3.
Kisses,
Olga xxx

Faith heaved a sigh of relief. She was mightily relieved that her last visit was going to be to a goodie, rather than a baddie. She hoped that the witch was going to behave herself and not slip back into her old habits, as she'd like to get out of this whole thing in one piece. Still, the address looked promisingly attractive. She couldn't possibly be murdered in fluffy slippers and a bathrobe. Or could she?

Chapter 17

'Oh to be a cloud, floating in the blue...'

Switzerland, Faith was pretty sure, was a long way away. This was made much more complicated by not knowing where she was right now. "Hmm, I don't know where I am," she mused, "where exactly I'm going, or how to get there."

She looked at Bus Bear expectantly. Bus Bear looked back at her until it became clear that he didn't know either. Faith looked around for a sign. She looked up to the sky for lifts and down at the grass for trapdoors. She checked her pockets and read the letter again. Nothing.

This was not how it worked. Surely an eagle should

appear and fly her to Switzerland, or the taxi driver should suddenly screech to a halt beside her to give her a lift. She waited for a few minutes, but nothing, absolutely *nothing* happened. It became glaringly obvious that she was on her own this time.

Faith sighed with frustration, beginning to feel a teensy bit irritated. How was she supposed to deliver the final letter without a little magic? Where was the tourist information turtle? The illuminated signs? The labels? After all, she was only human.

Faith lay back on the grass with a sigh and looked to the heavens above. The clouds were making creature shapes in the sky. She had always liked this game and had played it many times in her garden at home. There was a whale and a big fat man on a bike. That one looked like a rabbit and that one like a monster in a tutu... She yawned. All that exercise had exhausted her and she began to slip into a daydream. Clouds were floating by like fluffy bath bubbles. She sighed again. Faith liked bubble baths. She would pile up the frothy foam and sculpt beards and wigs. She plonked them on her head and made funny faces in the bathroom mirror. She loved the way she could balance a big chunk of bubbles on her fingers and then – *poof!* – blow them away.

She thought she would like to be a cloud, weightless and free, drifting here and there with the wind... She began to feel a bit faint, like the time when she had gone up in the London Eye and thought she would have to be sick in her rucksack, so she closed her eyes and tried to have a little doze.

It was about then that Faith began to rise off the ground. Could this really be happening? Yes, slowly but surely, she felt her body part company with the damp grass. "Oooh, er... what's going on?" she cried anxiously.

Up and up she floated, like a feather carried away on the breeze. Eventually she came to a stop, hovering in mid-air, hundreds of feet above the ground. Below her she saw fields laid out like patchwork. She could see the canyon and the valley. She could see the river and the forest and she could even see the flickering pink neon sign on top of Bo Peep's Kebab Palace.

She looked down at her hands and feet. They were misty white and barely there. Her heart filled with joy. "I'm a cloud!" she squealed with delight. "A real, proper cloud!"

She was astounded and amazed. She wondered how on earth it could ever have happened.

But really, truly, *secretly* of course, she knew precisely how it had happened.

Faith knew that she had made it happen, simply because she could. Just as you and I know exactly where to scratch an itch, Faith had known how to become a cloud. This was the first time, though, that it had happened, and Faith was fervently hoping that she wouldn't fall to a dramatic death when a huge gust of wind lifted her up and blew her clean across the sky. Beneath her, the earth rushed away and the sky became darker and darker.

Further and further she flew, until she was set adrift amongst an ocean of stars. She could hear distant voices, hundreds and thousands of whispered questions sent out into the night sky. It got louder and louder. Her head felt as if it would burst with the clamour when, as suddenly as it had started, it stopped.

Silence reigned supreme.

After a moment Faith said, "Hello? Is anybody there?" Her voice sounded different – echoey and oddly distant. "Am I near Switzerland yet?"

Gradually she began to drift downwards again, creeping slowly through the sky like golden syrup dripping off a spoon. This time she felt heavier, less wispy. She looked down at her hands. They were greyish rather than the snowy white they had been earlier. A wave of sadness washed over her like cold bathwater and she understood that she was becoming a rain-cloud.

Faith sank further and further down until she could see the landscape below clearly. This was definitely a different place. Ice-capped mountains punctuated green, lush meadows like dinosaur spikes. She could see the tiny figures of people perched on the hillside like daisies. Some of them were holding what looked like big shotguns.

"Look, Daddy," she heard one boy cry, "that one's shaped just like a little girl! Get it! Get it!"

Suddenly the air was filled with the sound of gunfire: *BOOM! BOOM! BOOM!*

What on earth...? Why were they shooting at the sky? Why were they shooting at her? She was a cloud!

"STOP!" she thundered, but her voice was caught on the wind and nobody but the birds could hear her.

As dozens of tiny pellets flew through her, Faith had a

strange sensation of dissolving, of falling apart slowly. She began to rain. She rained right into the enormous expanse of water below. She rained and she poured. Within a matter of seconds, Faith Smyth had completely disappeared.

Chapter 18

Shangri-La Surprise

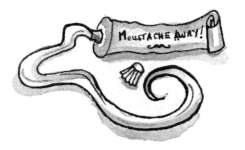

Faith felt strange, like she wasn't all there. But that was OK, because she wasn't. She was all around the lake in droplets, diluted like orange squash. Slowly, somewhere in the far corner of the lake, a tiny particle of Faith began to sing an odd tinkly tune. Another particle joined in, then another and another. Before long the song had built to a crescendo, a vibrating wave of sound that pulsed towards the centre of the lake. Millions of crystal droplets rushed together and, in a gush of bubbles, rebuilt Faith Smyth in the blink of an eye.

She swam to the surface and gasped for air. In the distance

she could see rowing boats tied to a pontoon. Wooden steps led up to a chrome diving board that shone like the sun. In the distance there was a white castle of fairy tale proportions.

'Well, this is *nice*,' thought Faith, as she swam effortlessly to the edge and climbed out.

There was a smart signpost attached to the pontoon.

**RESIDENTS ARE RESPECTFULLY REMINDED
THAT DIVE-BOMBING IS NOT ALLOWED
AS THE LOCH NESS MONSTER
SUFFERS TERRIBLY WITH HER NERVES.
THANK YOU FOR YOUR COOPERATION.
THE MANAGEMENT OF THE SHANGRI-LA HEALTH &
BEAUTY SPA.**

Another close shave, then. But here she was. She had made it at last.

As Faith dripped up the steps towards the castle she knew that she should be feeling relieved. She *should* be brimming with joy. Finally this strange, scary, life-threatening job was nearly over and she could go back home. She could go back to being ordinary Faith, safe and sound with her reliable books and regular snacks.

Hooray.

This *should* have made her feel pleased, but instead she felt strangely unsettled. Her walking became a reluctant shuffle. She felt the minutes of her adventure trickling away as if they were sand in an hourglass. She had an overwhelming urge to turn and run away despite the fact that she didn't belong here; here in this weird, wonderful place. Faith belonged in the real world. She could almost feel reality tugging at the hem of her school skirt. Now she came to think about it, she wasn't at all sure that she liked being ordinary; there didn't seem to be too many perks.

But it was too late for doubts, for she had reached the front entrance. Pushing open a set of tall glass doors, she entered a foyer. There were wafty green plants and trickly water features that made Faith want to go to the loo. Low, calming music played in the background. Faith went over to the reception desk and rang a small brass bell.

A gorilla dressed in a white tunic appeared. His name badge said 'Maurice' and he had unfortunate speech difficulties.

"Welcome to Thhangwi-La Health and Beauty Thpa; I am Mauwice. I hope you are enjoying our annual cloudbuthting fethtival entitled 'Thoot the clouds and make it wain'. How may I help you today?" He looked sympathetically at Faith, as if she obviously needed rather a lot of help.

Faith drew herself up to her full height. "I need to speak to Olga the witch," she announced in a confident voice. "My name is Faith Smyth and I have a confidential delivery for her eyes only."

Maurice leant forward over the desk and whispered behind his enormous hand, "At latht! Ith it her mouthtache-wemoving cweam?"

"No! It isn't!" cried Faith, shuddering at the thought of it. Yik and double yik. Maurice didn't try to hide his disappointment. "Oh, dear. Wighty-ho, follow me then."

Maurice led the way up a wide spiral staircase. Crystal chandeliers hung from the towering ceiling and fresh lilies posed on elegant stands. It was *very* posh. They walked down a corridor lined with dozens of identical shining white doors.

Eventually they stopped at a door marked 'Foot Heaven'.

Maurice knocked on the door and it swung open.

"Mth D'thpicable, you have a vithitor," he announced in hushed tones, waving Faith inside.

There before her lay Olga in all her glory. Faith knew it was Olga because it is difficult to miss a witch dressed in an all-in-one orange Lycra bodysuit and rainbow leg warmers. The pointy black hat was a dead giveaway too. Lying on a couch, listening to an iPod whilst having her toenails painted hot pink, Olga was blowing a big strawberry bubble. As she turned to look at Faith, it popped all over her pointy nose. Faith noted that the hair-removal cream delivery was long overdue.

"AAARRGGHH!" screeched Olga in horror, pointing a bony finger at Faith. "It's a *CHILD!*"

The lady who had been painting Olga's toes was now trying to pick the bubble gum out of the witch's moustache, but Olga forced her off. Panic was scrawled all over her face. "What do you want? How did you find me? Are you one of Gretel's cronies?"

"No, I most certainly am not," sighed Faith impatiently. "I'm not here to shove you in any microwaves, so you can just settle down and stop getting your knickers in a twist."

Olga relaxed back on to the couch and put her sunglasses back on. "So what do you want, then?" she asked in a bored voice.

Faith placed the letter carefully on Olga's lap. "I needed to give you back your letter. I needed to give them all back and now you're the only one left." She explained the whole story for the last time. Finally she said flatly, "And I've done what had to be done, so now it's time to go home."

"What?" Olga stared gormlessly at Faith and pulled her iPod earphones out. "What was that? What did you say?"

"Honestly!" exclaimed Faith crossly. "You didn't listen to a word I said, did you? I don't even know why Lancelot bothered!"

She turned to leave in disgust when Olga, in an unexpected burst of enthusiasm, suddenly leapt up and draped her arm cosily over Faith's shoulder. "Did you say Lancelot, as in *Sir* Lancelot? Oh, he is *well* fit! He's soooo handsome and brave and, well… just yummy. Did you say he was asking after me? Don't you think we'd make a lovely couple?" Olga was steering a bewildered Faith out of the door and up the corridor. Olga went on relentlessly, "You see, we met by moonlight (well, actually I was wearing my super-bright head torch, but it's the same thing) when he came to visit a friend of mine." Olga looked romantically into the distance and put her hand over her heart. "I knew there was something *incredible* between us from that moment on."

"Really?" asked Faith doubtfully, trying to disentangle herself from Olga's arm.

"Yes, definitely. It was the way he said, 'Please, please stop, you're blinding me!' Tone is everything, don't you think? A woman knows these things." Olga winked mysteriously.

"Who was he visiting?" asked Faith, desperate to change the subject.

"Why," she squealed, "that's where I'm taking you now, you silly-billy!" At this Olga swung open a set of double doors to reveal an enormous room. It was full of people Faith vaguely recognised, engrossed in discussions or sitting at desks working.

She passed a tall thin man with a tin whistle poking out of the top pocket of his moth-eaten suit. He looked fraught. He was typing out a newsletter headed 'The Pied Piper School for the Unusually Persistent'.

The first line read:

Dear parents,

I simply must insist that you collect your children after school. It is not funny any more. They won't go home and once again I find myself stressing the need for personal space...

A winged horse worked the room, handing out leaflets. He was wearing a rosette that said 'Got a question? Vote Equestrian'. Faith took one and had a read.

We believe in a government that stands up for
The important issues.

YES to mints, slow drivers and pooing in the street.
NO to cross little girls, flies and sudden loud noises
(except the ones that come from our bottoms).

She noticed a little blonde girl scribbling forcibly on a Post-it note:

Somebody — and I think it was probably a BEAR — has

stolen my fruits of the forest yoghurt and better put it back sharpish!
That goes for my moisturiser too, Daddy Bear!

She slapped it on a fridge door and stomped off gripping a wooden spoon.

Near the fireplace an enormous man was squashed into a chair, cheerily typing an email.

Dear Sir or Madam,

My name is Thor. I would like to work for the council recycling department. I think I would be good at this as I have lightning for melting and a big hammer for those items that are difficult to crush. I have passed an exam in art and I am also a god.

Faith noticed a group of pretty teenage girls in the corner, gossiping and drinking big mugs of tea. They were all wearing tiaras and one was clearly quite worked up, clutching a golden ball. Faith couldn't help but overhear her saying, "Then, *and you will not believe this*, he said, 'I don't think it's going to work with me being a frog and you being a princess! No offence, sweetie-pie,' he said, 'but you don't even know how to boil a slug!' What a nerve!" She dabbed at her eyes with a hankie and gave a big sigh. All the other princesses nodded sympathetically and took another biscuit from the tin.

Faith guessed that this was some sort of freaky drop-in centre for mythical characters. Olga steered Faith across the swirly carpet with a steely grip on her elbow. They headed for the corner of the room where an old lady was reading a newspaper by open French windows. The headline of her newspaper read:

GINGERBREAD MAN MISSING
IN EXTREME SPORTS TRAGEDY

"Oh, dear, how dreadful," tutted the old lady, without the slightest hint of regret. "Never mind, I'm sure it's all for the best." She took off her glasses and folded the newspaper in her lap.

Olga elbowed Faith forward and announced triumphantly, "Here you go, Hope, just like I promised. Good as my word; not even so much as a nibble."

Faith eyed Olga suspiciously. What was she up to?

The old lady looked up at Faith and gave a wide smile that stretched all the way to her crinkly, twinkly blue eyes. "Hello, my dear. Goodness – you're taller than I remember. Barley sugar?" She held out a paper bag full of shiny orange sweets.

"Yes, please," said Faith, more out of politeness than hunger. As she unwrapped the sweet, Faith wondered who this one might be. Maybe she was the grandmother from Little Red Riding Hood, or maybe she was Jack and the Beanstalk's mother. Most importantly, she seemed harmless enough, which made a nice change.

All at once the old lady's attention switched to Faith's blazer pocket. "Well, blow me over with a phoenix feather!" she announced loudly, "if it isn't my old friend Bartleby Barsupicle! It certainly has been a while. How *are* you, my dear boy?"

As a flummoxed Faith looked around, she couldn't help but notice that her pocket had begun to billow smoke. She yanked out BB like a hot potato and held him by the ear fluff. A new label was flapping around his neck. It said quite clearly:

WOTCHA HOPE

149

Chapter 19

Faith, Hope and Clarity

Jigsaws had never been Faith's speciality. She'd get the pieces out and dutifully arrange them on the carpet, but they always seemed to be just a jumbled collection of badly fitting bits. She generally needed some help to piece the big picture together and this was going to be no exception.

She peered at the old lady suspiciously. "Do I know you?"

But of course, way down inside, Faith suspected she already knew the answer, just as she had known how to become a cloud. The fact was that she just wasn't ready to face up to it yet.

Hope avoided the question and heaved herself up out of the chair, picking up her walking stick. "Shall we go for a walk in the garden? The roses are so lovely at this time of year."

Faith trailed behind Hope. The two of them followed a winding brick path through the most beautiful perfumed rose garden. For some reason that Faith couldn't explain, she felt overwhelmed by the feeling that she had been here before. Even odder than that, it felt... nice; it felt like *home*. This was all getting a bit out of hand. Something was going on, but the pieces wouldn't fit together.

Hope sat down on a bench, unwrapped another barley sugar and popped it in her mouth. She rattled it around her teeth for a while, watching Faith with a keen interest. Eventually she casually asked, "So. Recognise anything?"

Faith nodded cautiously.

She perched on the sun-warmed bench next to Hope and they sat in silence for a while, looking at the roses. Eventually it was Faith who broke the silence. "I'm here for a reason, aren't I?" she murmured quietly, almost too quietly to be heard. "It's no accident, is it?"

"No, Faith, it's no accident." Hope put the bag of sweets

back in her handbag and snapped it shut. "Lancelot was under strict orders."

Faith's memory whizzed back to her first meeting with Lancelot. What was it he had said? *"Ah, my dear Faith, how good to see you."*

"Shakespeare, a great friend of mine," Hope continued, "once wrote: 'Some are born great, some achieve greatness and others have greatness thrust upon them'. You, Faith Smyth, are all three."

Faith felt awkward. "I think you must have me confused with someone else. I'm just an ordinary little girl. I have trouble keeping my hair-slides in, so I doubt I could handle greatness." She got up to leave. "It's been very nice meeting you, though, and thanks for the sweet, but now all the letters are back safe and sound, I think it's probably time that I went home."

Hope sighed and leant on her stick. "Faith, maybe I should get straight to the point. Were you, or were you not, a cloud earlier on?"

Faith nodded reluctantly, desperately wondering how Hope could have known this bit of information.

"Now, did you wonder how you could do that? It's not

really very ordinary, is it?" Faith had to admit that it wasn't your usual everyday thing to do.

Hope smiled broadly and looked Faith in the eye. "Young lady, I think you know that you are *far* from ordinary."

And she was right, of course. Faith and Hope. Hope and Faith. Faith didn't know exactly what it meant, but she knew it meant something important. Something from a time long ago, far away.

"Have you ever wondered about your name, *Faith Smyth*? Have you ever said it quickly?" queried Hope. Faith returned a blank stare.

Hope sighed and rolled her eyes to the heavens. "Dearie me, this is obviously going to be harder than I thought. Faith Smyth? *Faith's Myth*?"

Faith's thoughts raced. She kept starting sentences but was lost for words. Finally she said, "Are you trying to tell me that this is the end of my story? And that none of this," she waved her hand around, "has been real?"

Hope chuckled. "Oh, it's real enough, all right. Real as rhubarb. And this isn't the end. There is more; much, *much* more." Hope opened her handbag again and took out a photograph.

It was a picture of a christening. Faith looked closer. It was *her* christening! There were her parents and all of her aunts and uncles. At the front was a tiny baby in a Moses basket, clutching a small blue bear. Right at the back of the photograph, in the far corner, was an old lady with a smile that stretched all the way to her twinkly, crinkly blue eyes – Dad's great-aunt Hope. Bingo! Faith *knew* they'd met before!

The old lady folded her hands in her lap. "Faith, I need you to be very brave now, because what I am about to tell you will change your life forever and nothing will ever be the same again. Are you ready?"

Faith wasn't at all sure she was ready, but she nodded anyway.

Hope rearranged her petticoats, cleared her throat and went on. "You are a special child, Faith, a *very* special child. You have a purpose, a destiny that must be filled, a job to do. Do you know what the name 'Faith' means?"

Faith thought back to the key ring she had bought with her holiday money in Cornwall last summer. It had explained it all, neatly encased in plastic. "Erm... is it from a Latin word? I think it means 'to believe' or 'to trust'.

Something like that."

"Full marks, young lady. Very impressive. However, in your case, Faith is more than a name." Hope took a deep breath and continued; "Faith Smyth, YOU are the most important cog in the storytelling machine. You are the rock upon which all make-believe is built. You are not in any way ordinary; you are *extra*ordinary. To put it simply, without your help, people will stop believing in stories. Fairy tales, folklore, legends, myths, fables – all of them. They will simply disappear – *poof!* – as will we. Stories won't matter any more. The world will be about facts and facts alone."

"But facts are important, aren't they?" said Faith "Aren't they the truth?"

"Yes, dear, facts are very important," said Hope with a smile. "But heartfelt belief is a wonderful thing too. Once upon a time this used to be a very important idea, but not so much these days. The balance has shifted and we are in grave danger of becoming extinct." She patted Faith's hand. "There's a lot of work to be done, and only you can save us."

Faith remembered BB's parcel label in the pirate dungeon:

'*Without Faith there can be no Hope*'.

This was rather a lot to take in. "But I'm just a little girl!" said Faith. "Isn't this a job for somebody more grown up? Somebody with qualifications? I can't even drive yet! I mean, I've only just learnt how to make toast!"

"Faith, you are an old soul. You were born at the dawn of time, millions of years ago like the stars." Hope reached into her handbag again and pulled out a silver-wrought hand mirror. She held it up to Faith's face. "The little girl you see before you is simply your most recent adventure. You are older than you think."

Whilst Faith looked at her wild hair and freckles in the murky mirror, Hope continued. "These are dark times for us all, my dear. People are not so ready to trust in us these days, and when they stop believing… well, that's a sticky end for any mythical character." Faith remembered the Tooth Fairy's words; hadn't she said that too?

Hope returned the ancient mirror to her bag. "You could have stayed at home with us here, but you insisted on going undercover to try and understand human beings, to understand why they needed us. You wanted to know how it felt to be lonely and afraid, to need stories to cheer you up. So you were born into a human family – a real humdinger of one as well!" Hope chuckled to herself. "No wonder you felt so different. I sent BB in after you as protection, as goodness only knows being a real person is terribly hard at times. But those in the know have been watching and waiting for the time you were ready to return home. It has been foretold, you know."

Wow! This was definitely more impressive than Jasmine Squire's pony club rosettes. "But you said that Lancelot was under strict orders. How did he know I was ready?"

Hope put her arm around Faith's shoulder and smiled kindly. "He didn't; he just gave you a nudge. You were the one who overcame your fear and faced up to the challenge. You were the one who defended the truth and came back of your own free will. Prepared to help, whatever the cost, you stepped into the filing cabinet. You had faith in the cause and, eventually, in yourself."

Faith looked around at the beautiful roses and breathed in their delicate scent. She glanced over to the French windows on the other side of the garden. Dozens of expectant faces were pressed up against the window, watching anxiously for good news.

"What about the Gingerbread Man? Was he in on it?"

"Certainly not. There's a rotten egg in every basket," Hope said, smiling. "Fortunately for us, he didn't realise who he was up against."

Faith looked down thoughtfully at her christening photograph. She was wondering with a guilty twinge if her mum and dad were missing her. She reassured herself that, on balance, probably not, as they hadn't *really* noticed her when she *was* there.

Then something very odd began to happen. The figures of the old lady, the small blue bear and the baby began to slowly fade from the photograph until all that was left was an empty Moses basket and a bunch of confused-looking relatives. They didn't look upset, rather more as if they couldn't remember where they'd left their car keys. It was as if she had never been there at all.

Faith no longer felt guilty or afraid or lonely or different. Instead she felt brave and wanted and important and *necessary*. In fact, it was fair to say that she felt bingo blooming brilliant! The final pieces of the jigsaw slotted together – *clunk* – and she was back where she rightfully belonged.

"When I was a cloud," murmured Faith dreamily, "way up in the heavens, I heard millions of voices asking questions." She giggled to herself. How could she have forgotten the one and only answer to all of them? "Have faith." She took Hope's arm and helped her up from the garden bench.

"We are all depending on you. You will stay this time, won't you, Faith?" asked Hope in an anxious voice. "You do remember, don't you?"

Faith smiled a smile as old as the universe itself and squeezed her hand. "Well, it's all a bit hazy, but I'm definitely back for good. After all, if it's been foretold, then who am I to argue?" Hope gave Faith's hand a satisfied pat, heaved herself up on her stick and began to walk back to the common room.

"Hang on a minute!" said Faith, "What exactly *is it* that I am supposed to do?"

Hope turned around and pushed her spectacles up higher on her nose. "Oh, don't worry, dear, it'll come to you." And with that she was gone.

Faith took BB out of her pocket. She looked him square in the buttons and said determinedly, "Well, Bus Bear, or Bartleby Barsupicle, or whatever your real name is, someone's got to stop the mythical world from falling apart, and apparently we are the best people for the job. There's no time to waste!"

She picked a beautiful crimson rose and tucked it behind her ear. Faith was a true beauty; inside and out. A new parcel label appeared around BB's neck:

GO GET 'EM, GIRL!

Acknowledgements

My thanks to the following: Mum, Dad and Helen for their love and wisdom; Toots and Geoff for their encouragement; Jane, Gill, Rachel and Paula for their cheerful support across the kitchen table; the children and staff of Filleigh Primary School; 'That New Place' for the electricity; and the delightful Fran at Boxer for her enthusiasm and expertise. My biggest thanks are to Julien, Daisy and Maya, who taught me everything I know.